MW00789823

The Keeper

AMISH COUNTRY BRIDES

Jennifer Spredemann

© 2021

Copyright 2021 by Jennifer Spredemann, J.E.B. Spredemann

All rights reserved. No part of this work/book may be copied, transmitted, or stored in any form or by any means, except for brief quotations in printed reviews, without prior written consent from the authors/publisher.

All incidents and characters in this book are completely fictional and derived by the author's imagination. Any resemblance to actual incidents and persons living or dead are purely coincidental.

Published in Indiana by *Blessed Publishing*.

www.jenniferspredemann.com

All Scripture quotations are taken from the *King James Version* of the *Holy Bible*.

Cover design by *iCreate Designs* ©

ISBN: 978-1-940492-59-9
10 9 8 7 6 5 4 3 2 1

Get a FREE short story as my thank you gift to you
when you sign up for my newsletter here:
www.jenniferspredemann.com

BOOKS by JENNIFER SPREDEMANN

AMISH BY ACCIDENT TRILOGY
Amish by Accident
*Englisch on Purpose (*Prequel to *Amish by Accident)*
*Christmas in Paradise (*Sequel to *Amish by Accident)* (co-authored with Brandi Gabriel)

AMISH SECRETS SERIES
An Unforgivable Secret - Amish Secrets 1
A Secret Encounter - Amish Secrets 2
A Secret of the Heart - Amish Secrets 3
An Undeniable Secret - Amish Secrets 4
A Secret Sacrifice - Amish Secrets 5 (co-authored with Brandi Gabriel)
A Secret of the Soul - Amish Secrets 6
A Secret Christmas – Amish Secrets 2.5 (co-authored with Brandi Gabriel)

AMISH BIBLE ROMANCES
An Amish Reward (Isaac)
An Amish Deception (Jacob)
An Amish Honor (Joseph)
An Amish Blessing (Ruth)
An Amish Betrayal (David)

Unofficial Glossary
of Pennsylvania Dutch Words

Ach – Oh

Aenti – Aunt

Boppli/Bopplin – Baby/Babies

Bruder/Brieder – Brother/Brothers

Chust – Just

Daed/Dat – Dad

Dawdi – Grandfather

Dawdi haus – A small dwelling typically used for grandparents

Denki – Thanks

Der Herr – The Lord

Dochder(n) – Daughter(s)

Dummkopp – Dummy

Englischer – A non-Amish person

Ferhoodled – Crazy, scatterbrained, mind is elsewhere

Fraa – Wife/Missus

G'may – Members of an Amish fellowship

Gott – God

Gross sohn – Grandson

Gut – Good

Guten tag – Good day, good morning

Herr – Mister/Lord

Jah – Yes

Kapp – Amish head covering

Kinner – Children

Kumm – Come

Maed/Maedel – Girls/Girl

Mamm – Mom

Rumspringa – Running around period for Amish youth

Schatzi – Sweetheart

Schweschder(n) – Sister(s)

Sohn – Son

Wunderbaar – Wonderful

Author's Note

The Amish/Mennonite people and their communities differ one from another. There are, in fact, no two Amish communities exactly alike. It is this premise on which this book is written. I have taken cautious steps to assure the authenticity of Amish practices and customs. Old Order Amish and New Order Amish may be portrayed in this work of fiction and may differ from some communities. Although the book may be set in a certain locality, the practices featured in the book may not necessarily reflect that particular district's beliefs or culture. This book is purely fictional and built around a fictional community, even though you may see similarities to real-life people, practices, and occurrences.

We, as *Englischers*, can learn a lot from the Plain People and their simple way of life. Their hard work, close-knit family life, and concern for others are to be applauded. As the Lord wills, may this special culture continue to be respected and remain so for many centuries to come, and may the light of God's salvation reach their hearts.

ONE

Hot fury seeped through Joshua Beachy's veins as he marched into the kitchen, then paced the empty space. It couldn't be true, could it? Because if it was...

Disbelief pervaded his thoughts as he plunked his hide into a dining room chair. One of the chairs his family had purchased from Lambright's Furniture. The place where he'd met and began a friendship with timid Lissa Lambright.

Ach, Lissa. If what his older brother Josiah had said over the phone was true, a tough decision would have to be made regarding their courting relationship. He feared the worst.

He tapped his foot and the sound reverberated off the walls of his folks' sparse farmhouse. Being one of the youngest, he could remember the time when this house was filled with his siblings' voices, and they all still lived at home. Now, it was just him, Justin, *Mamm*, and *Daed*.

Why hadn't *Mamm* and *Daed* said anything to him about their plans to move away? Sure, he'd heard them toss the idea around, but he never actually thought his parents would seriously consider packing up and moving to Indiana.

As soon as he confirmed the truth of the matter with his folks, he and Lissa would need to have a heart-to-heart. Dread filled him at just the thought. Lissa wasn't good with change. He'd noticed her insecurities at the beginning of their courtship, but he'd never minded it. He enjoyed being wanted, needed. *Jah*, this would surely rock her world. And not in a good way.

He jumped up the moment he heard buggy wheels crunching on the gravel driveway. He blew through the door and made a beeline for the hitching post.

"Are we moving to Indiana?" The words flew out of his mouth. Was his heart thumping double-time?

Mamm's eyes widened as she shared a look with *Daed*. *Daed* frowned in return.

"We planned to have a family meeting tonight," *Daed* said.

"So, it's true then?"

His father nodded once as he began to unharness

their mare. "*Chust* got back from the realtor's office."

Joshua eyed the folder *Mamm* now carried to the house, and his shoulders finally sunk under the weight of the news. This was real. They were really moving to Indiana. His heart clenched. "What about Lissa?" He barely uttered the words through his tight throat, which seemed to be constricting more with each second.

At first, their courtship had been a secret like many in the *g'may*, but they'd since become more open. It was too difficult to keep things hush-hush when you were eager to be with someone. Joshua had known the first time he'd visited the furniture store alone that Lissa's father suspected something.

"I'm sorry, *sohn*."

He knew the look in *Daed's* eye meant there would be no negotiating. They'd already made up their minds.

Either he moved to Indiana with his folks, or he stayed here alone. *Nee*, not alone. With Lissa. Because he knew without a doubt she wouldn't be willing to move with him. Yet, the thought of staying and raising a family without having his folks nearby evoked emotions he didn't want to identify.

"I will need your help," *Daed* said. "There will be a lot of work that will need to be done when we purchase a place. I'm counting on you. Your *aldi* will understand. You can always move back later if you choose to raise a family here in Pennsylvania."

"Justin's going too, right?"

"Eventually. He'll look after the house until it sells. After that, he'll make his way to Indiana as well."

Which meant he and *Daed* would be responsible for preparing the fields and planting new crops and whatnot. It would be a big job for just the two of them, depending on how much land *Daed* planned to purchase. But he suspected his brothers, Josiah and Jaden, would lend a hand if necessary.

That was the bright spot in all this mess. He'd get to see his older brothers again and meet his newest nieces and nephews. But before then, he needed to speak with Lissa.

"When will we leave?" The words clogged Joshua's throat, making him sound like a frog to his own ears.

"First thing next week."

So, one more meeting with the *g'may*. One more singing and buggy ride to Lissa Lambright's. One more time to hold her in his arms. That was, if she let him. And that was a big "if," considering how upset she'd likely be.

He sighed again. How would the leaders feel about this? Chances are, if his folks had planned this far, the leaders already knew their intentions. No doubt some in the *g'may* would be disgruntled. Their family had been a staple in this community for several generations.

This was all his brother Josiah's fault. If he hadn't left during his *rumspringa* and if he hadn't created the unnecessary havoc in their family, they'd *all* still be here. It was mind-boggling how one person's decisions unwittingly affected so many others' lives.

Joshua growled under his breath. He planned to have words with his older brother.

~

"You'll never believe who's moving out this way." Martha Miller couldn't hide her grin if she duct taped her lips together.

Susan rolled her eyes at her older sister. Like a new family moving into the community was exciting news. "No idea."

"*Ach*, you're no fun." She bounced one of her toddler twins on her knee. "Is she, Nancy? *Nee*, your *aenti* Susan is a stick-in-the-mud these days."

Her sister let the little one down when she reached for her toy on the floor. "Fine, I'll tell you. Alvin and Ada Beachy." Martha's grin widened even further. "And I hear Joshua and Justin are coming too." She practically sang the words.

Susan snorted. "Why would I care about that?"

"You need someone to put a smile on your face. You're such a grump nowadays."

"Believe me, it won't be one of them." She'd already had her share of buggy rides home with overeager immature Amish males. She had no interest in a repeat performance.

"Well, I know I already got the cutest one, but the others aren't bad to look at."

"I think Nora would challenge you on that one." Susan laughed out loud, then stood from the table. "And, handsome or not, I'm not interested."

"How do you expect to find yourself a husband if you always have a sour disposition? Men aren't attracted to that sort of thing." This, coming from Martha? She'd been the one with the sour disposition until Jaden came along and swept her off her feet. Now, she seemed to be Miss Happy-Go-Lucky. It was enough to make Susan wretch.

"There's more to life than attracting a man, Martha. You're beginning to sound like Emily. Maybe I don't *want* to get married." The statement wasn't exactly true, although she was definitely in no hurry to utter her lifelong vows.

Martha huffed. "Whyever not? Don't you want *bopplin*?"

"Not anytime soon."

"By the time you make up your mind, all the good ones will be taken and you'll be too old to bear *kinner*."

Susan shrugged. "If that happens, so be it. There's nothing wrong with staying single, is there?"

"No, not if that's what God wants for you. I just couldn't imagine not having Jaden and the twins in my life. I get so much joy from them."

Susan was tempted to snicker, but she held back. "You were mad at Jaden last week," she reminded her sister.

"I didn't say my life was perfect. It doesn't have to be. I don't think perfection exists in any marriage with two imperfect people. We all have our issues." She rifled through the diaper bag and handed the baby a toy. "And just so you know, I'd marry Jaden again in a heartbeat."

Just then, Jaden stuck his head through the doorway. "Martha, you ready to go yet? I've got a stack of papers to correct as high as *Daed's* silo waiting for me at home." Jaden stepped inside with little Nelson.

"I thought you were staying for supper." Susan eyed her sister.

"Not today. We just had to stop by to drop off

Mamm's pans that I borrowed." Martha scooped up the baby. "I brought cookies. You better grab a couple before Nathaniel eats them all."

"Did I hear someone say they made cookies for me?" Nathaniel appeared out of nowhere and hastened toward the kitchen.

Susan jumped up to snatch one and Martha laughed. "They are for everyone, *bruder*. Make sure you share," Martha said.

"Do I have to? These are delicious." Nathaniel groaned around a bite of cookie. "Jaden, you're a blessed man."

Jaden waggled his eyebrows and kissed the *boppli* in his arms. "Don't I know it."

Martha charged over to Nathaniel and planted a loud kiss on his cheek. "*Denki, bruder*. I think that's the nicest thing you've ever said about me."

"Well, don't let it go to your head," Nathaniel teased.

"Hey, it's too bad Jaden's folks don't have any available *dochdern*. We could get Nathaniel married off too." Martha shared a conspiratorial look with Jaden. "He needs a *gut* woman."

"Oh, no. Not you too. Have you been talking to Silas and Paul?" Nathaniel pointed a cookie at her. "And I take back my compliment now."

"You can't take back a compliment." Martha insisted. "And to answer your question, no, I have not been conspiring with our *brieder*. I was simply making an observation."

"Well, if I recall correctly, *you* were in no rush to get married either," Nathaniel remarked. "At least, not until..." He nodded toward the *bopplin*.

"Nathaniel Miller!" *Mamm* joined the group in the kitchen, and promptly swatted Nathaniel with a dish towel. "You know better than to speak of that."

"Uh, Martha?" Jaden tapped his foot and gestured toward the door, suddenly looking uncomfortable. "Let's go now?"

Nathaniel chuckled. "Escaping the heat, *bruder*?"

Jaden chortled. "Maybe I just want to spark more." He raised an eyebrow toward his wife.

Mamm and Susan both gasped. When had her quiet brother-in-law become so bold?

Martha, with cheeks flaming, promptly clutched Jaden's shirt sleeve and ushered him to the door. "We're leaving now."

Susan laughed as her *schweschder* and brother-in-law stepped outside with the twins. No doubt, her *schweschder* was about to give her brother-in-law a talking to.

"Why didn't you swat *him* with the towel?"

Nathaniel turned toward their *mamm,* thumbing over his shoulder to where Jaden had just escaped.

"I should have. That boy..." *Mamm* huffed. "Well, at least they're married now."

"And will probably have another one on the way soon, by the sound of it," Nathaniel teased.

"I've had enough of your comments for one day, *sohn,*" *Mamm* warned.

Susan shook her head.

"Susan, did you get that laundry off the line yet? It needs to be folded and put away before we start on supper," *Mamm* reminded.

An inward groan escaped Susan's lips unbidden, resulting in a displeased look from *Mamm.* "I thought you wanted me to pick more produce for Emily's roadside stand?" It technically wasn't Emily's stand anymore, not since her younger *schweschder* had married the widower Titus Troyer. But they'd called it Emily's for so long, it had become a habit.

"You haven't done that yet?" *Mamm* tsked. "Well, you better get a move on then, because I'll need your help with supper and cutting up the fruit for the pies we're making for church tomorrow."

"When are the Beachys coming?" Nathaniel asked *Mamm.* "Martha said Alvin and Ada are moving into the community."

Mamm's eyes widened. "Here? To Bontrager's district?"

"That's what Jaden said. They're moving here since Detweiler's *g'may* is so strict. Since they know people in both communities, they figured ours would be the wiser choice even though their family attends Detweiler's."

Susan tried not to listen as she fetched the laundry basket.

"It wonders me if they'll consider the property across the road? Just went up for sale last week, *Dat* said." *Mamm* turned her attention to Susan. "What are you still doing inside, *maedel*? Get a move on. That laundry isn't going to fold itself."

Ach. Ever since Emily and Martha had moved out, it seemed like the chores were never-ending. She hurried outside and yanked the laundry off the line in frustration.

It was indeed true that many hands made light work. It was too bad the hands were becoming fewer every year, it seemed. With her luck, Nathaniel would be finding himself a *fraa* soon and Susan would be left with his chores too. The thought was almost enough to make her scream.

She thought about the Beachys' potentially moving close by.

On the bright side, if the Beachy parents did purchase the property across the street, there was a *gut* chance her older sister would be around more. Susan knew, from what Martha had said in the past, that Jaden had been pretty close with his folks and worked side by side with his father in their cornfield for most of his growing-up years. He still spoke of his time at home with fondness.

She couldn't help but wonder why Jaden wasn't a farmer, since he enjoyed it so much. He'd come to Indiana to fill a teaching position, but Susan suspected his move had a lot more to do with courting Martha than a job.

She noticed a car driving by as she folded a pair of Nathaniel's trousers and dropped them into the basket. The car's reflection of the sun nearly blinded her until it passed. The vehicle was completely open on the top like the Swiss Amish buggies. Fun music blared from the vehicle and a couple of *Englisch* girls near her own age had loose hair whipping around them in the breeze. She suspected their sunglasses kept the unruly tresses out of their eyes.

Oh, to be so carefree! Just driving around on a Saturday without a mounting list of chores to be completed. What would it be like to let her hair fly all around her while driving in a car? What would it be like to turn on a radio and listen to whatever tickled her fancy? What would it be like to not have to suffer through the hot summer months, but instead be inside enjoying cool air conditioning?

What would it be like to be *Englisch*? She closed her eyes and tried to picture herself in *Englisch* clothes, living in an *Englisch* home, working an *Englisch* job. *Ach*, the prospect sounded like absolute heaven.

TWO

Joshua had no idea how long he'd be in Lambright's Furniture store, so he opted for securing the reins to the hitching post, as opposed to letting his horse graze in the small paddock behind the building. Sometimes Lissa was busy with customers and she couldn't get away. Although she mostly tended to the establishment's clerical duties in the back office, her father occasionally called on her to help out with a customer if he and Lissa's brother Terry were occupied.

Whatever the case today, Joshua had to speak with her. If she was busy, then he'd have to wait. All he knew was that he *needed* to tell Lissa his news before it was announced at meeting tomorrow. It wouldn't be right for her to hear the news secondhand and be caught unawares. He expected it would be jarring enough coming from him.

A wall of frigid air slammed Joshua's face the

moment he stepped through the entrance. Since Lissa's father had partnered with an *Englischer* when he purchased the store, he was allowed to use air conditioning. *Ach*, it felt nice compared to the current temperatures outside. Joshua had broken into a sweat on just the ride over. The humidity in Pennsylvania could get rough this time of year.

"Joshua Beachy, what brings you by today?" Lissa's chipper father greeted him. "I trust the family is well."

"Hello, Ron. *Jah*, we are all well." He glanced around the store. "Is Lissa in?"

Ron grimaced. "Actually, she's out of town until the end of next week. Her *schweschder* had her *boppli* yesterday." He brightened at the statement. Another baby in the family was always a joyous occasion.

Joshua scratched his cheek. *Ach*, he'd forgotten she'd mentioned something about going to visit her sister in New York, but that was to be a couple of weeks away yet.

"The baby arrived a little early," Ron explained.

Joshua blew out a breath. "Okay, then. Is there a phone number I can reach her at?"

"Afraid not. At least not yet. You see, they were in the middle of switching out the phone lines. But Lissa said she'd call when she gets a chance. I expect she'll have the new number then."

Right. And he'd probably be halfway to Indiana at that time.

"If I leave a letter for her, could you see that she gets it?"

Ron nodded. "I can do that."

"Okay. I'll give it to you at church tomorrow."

"Very well." He nodded. "And let your father know I'm looking forward to his corn harvest this year."

Except there wouldn't be any corn harvest here in Pennsylvania this year, but Joshua had no desire to explain that to Lissa's father right now. He'd rather let *Daed* discuss that among the men at church tomorrow.

"*Denki.*" Joshua lifted a hand in departure as he stepped back into the stifling heat. Hopefully, the weather in southeastern Indiana would be more pleasant.

Twenty minutes later, he arrived back at home. Pen in hand, he sat down at *Daed's* desk with a sheet of lined paper. He felt cold-hearted breaking up with her over a letter. *Breaking up? Jah*, that was basically what it would amount to.

Joshua liked Lissa a lot and enjoyed her company, but he was nowhere near the marrying stage, even though she'd hinted at it a couple of times. If he were honest with himself, he'd admit there had always been something missing in their relationship. He couldn't even pinpoint what it was, really. Maybe a lack of passion? Truly, he felt like they were just friends more than anything, even though they had kissed a few times.

He didn't feel love for her, but he *did* care for her. He figured that if they had married in the future, the feelings of love would eventually come. Or, at least, he hoped they would.

The worst part about this whole ordeal was that it would devastate Lissa, and that tore him up inside. He'd always been sensitive to others' needs. He hated that he would be the cause of another person's inner turmoil.

He stared at the paper until his eyes blurred. What on earth was he supposed to write? *Hey, Lissa. It was nice knowing you. I moved away to Indiana and I probably won't see you again for several years, if at all.*

He shook his head. *Nee*, that would never work. A letter seemed so inadequate, so impersonal. He really needed to be face-to-face to have a heart-to-heart. He half-smiled at his silly musings, but the truth remained.

He took a deep breath and bowed his head. "Lord, I really need some guidance here. Please show me what to write to Lissa because I honestly have no clue. You know what she needs to hear."

He picked up the pen once again and the words began to flow.

~

"It's time, *sohn*." *Daed's* hand rested on Joshua's shoulder as they watched their driver load up the last of the horses into the trailer.

Joshua glanced back toward the house. He was going to miss this place like crazy. Being the youngest of the siblings, he always thought he'd be the one to inherit this old house and the property it sat on. Instead, it would likely be sold to strangers, or possibly someone in the *g'may* looking for a larger home. At this moment in time, he wished he had one of those disposable cameras so he could have photos of the place. Maybe he'd suggest that to his brother Justin, since he'd be staying on a little longer yet.

"You ready?" He heard the enthusiasm in *Daed's* voice. If only he could muster some as well.

"Ready as I'll ever be, I suppose. I just wish I could have talked to Lissa in person."

"But you left her a letter, ain't so?"

"*Jah*, with Ron. I hope he gives it to her." He looked down their driveway, longing for Lissa to appear. If only he could make it happen by sheer will, but maybe it wasn't meant to be. A letter just seemed like a lousy way to say goodbye.

"I'm sure and certain he will." His father stepped toward the awaiting vehicle. They'd already said their goodbyes. "*Kumm,* now. We can't keep the driver waiting any longer."

Joshua sighed. "Okay, let's go then."

He followed his father and climbed into the SUV. He reached for the pillow he'd tossed in earlier and settled in for a long ride to Indiana.

THREE

Moonlight cast shadows on Susan's wall, when she thought it to be morning already. Either way, she was wide awake, so no sense attempting to extend her beauty sleep. Not that it would help, according to Nathaniel. She hadn't let his thoughtless comment discourage her, since she knew he'd meant it in jest. One thing her brothers were good at was teasing.

She squinted, attempting to make out the time on her windup clock. Almost four, which meant she had an hour before anyone else would be up and around. If she tiptoed down the stairs, would she be able to indulge in a glass of cold lemonade without waking the others? Probably.

After seeing that Nathaniel's room was dark, she released a sigh. Since the two of them were the only remaining adult children in the house, she didn't have to worry about waking the others. She missed days of old when her older brothers Silas and Paul were still living at home. She missed their teasing and rivalry. She missed the smiles they'd always brought to her face. Why did things have to change?

She hurried to the kitchen and pulled the pitcher from the refrigerator, then filled a glass, her mouth salivating in anticipation. Was she really that parched? She refrained from lighting a lantern and plunked herself down in *Dat's* chair at the head of the table, allowing the refreshing beverage to delight her tastebuds and trickle down her throat. *Ach*, the tangy sweetness hit the spot.

The curtains fluttered in the breeze filtering through the open window. Was it her imagination, or did she hear faint voices? Strange. What were *Dat* and Nathaniel doing outside at this hour? She neared the window to confirm she wasn't losing her mind. Just as she was about to lower her ear to the screen, the door creaked open.

Oh no. She glanced down at herself. Hair undone, nightgown, head uncovered. *Ach.* She'd catch a disapproving look from *Dat* for sure and certain.

Except, one of the voices entering her home didn't belong to *Dat* or Nathaniel. Was it too late to make a dash for her room without being noticed? *Jah.*

She considered diving under the table, but then what? If *Dat* and whoever it was sat down, that would just be awkward. She imagined herself crawling around on the floor near everyone's feet and being accidentally kicked. That would surely be the most embarrassing thing ever. But there wasn't anywhere else to hide. Should she just come out and show her face or...?

"Susan? Is that you in there, *dochder*?" *Dat* held up a lantern.

She thrust her drink onto the table and quickly crossed her arms over her chest. "Uh, *jah*. I was just fetching a drink. I didn't know anyone was awake. Or that you had a visitor."

"Visitors," *Dat* remarked. Instead of looking chagrined, his eyes danced with amusement.

She didn't think this situation was funny in the least.

He shined the light on their visitors. "The Beachys came into town early."

Sure enough, Alvin, Ada, and a young man whom she suspected to be either Joshua or Justin stood, eyes wide, taking in her attire. Did their son just smirk at her? The nerve!

Her gaze bounced to each of them, then back to her father. Her face must be aflame. Fortunately, all was dark except for the lantern's glow.

"I'll...I'll go change and..." She gestured toward her room, then spun around and shot up the stairs before any comments were made.

It wasn't until she arrived safely behind her closed door, that she realized she'd been too *ferhoodled* to even greet their visitors properly.

What seemed to start out as a *wunderbaar* day had just sunk to an all-time low. She should have stayed in bed.

~

Oh. My. Word.

Jaden hadn't been kidding when he'd said there were pretty girls in Bontrager's district. *Wow.*

Joshua ran his hand over his stubbled chin, unable to fasten his jaw to his upper lip. He hadn't known his folks and Susan's father had been watching him as his riveted gaze followed the gorgeous model...er, uh, *maedel* up the staircase—until *Daed* cleared his throat, and Joshua discovered all eyes were on him.

"I...uh." He snapped his mouth shut. *Jah*, he needed to stop talking before he said something really *dumm.*

"And *that* was my middle *dochder*, Susan," her father informed them. "Emily, our youngest, married last year and moved out. It is only Susan, our youngest

24

son, Nathaniel, their *mudder*, and me living here now. Plenty of room yet. So, you are welcome to stay in our *dawdi haus* as long as you need to."

Since Joshua's *bruder* Jaden and his *fraa* had been married by the local justice of the peace, their family hadn't attended their wedding. And while some of the Miller family had traveled to Pennsylvania to visit for Christmas a few years back, their entire clan hadn't been present. Because, if Susan had been, Joshua *would have* remembered her.

Of course, he imagined she'd look quite different with her hair properly secured and attired in a traditional cape dress. But still.

Her father walked to an interior door, which, Joshua guessed, led to the *dawdi haus*. "There are two small bedrooms, so I think it should be adequate."

Two bedrooms, which meant he and Justin would have to share a room once his *bruder* arrived. It would feel like old times, in that respect.

"If you're tired, feel free to relax. I'm sure the journey must've been exhausting." *Herr* Miller gestured inside the small dwelling.

Joshua had been tired up until a few minutes ago. But now? There was no way he'd be able to get a wink of sleep knowing Susan Miller would be up and about soon.

How quickly his melancholy mood had shifted. All of a sudden, the Hoosier state didn't seem like such a bad place to live after all.

FOUR

Susan glanced behind her as she and *Mamm* prepared breakfast for their family and the Beachys. *Gut,* handsome Joshua—she'd learned his name when *Dat* mentioned it to *Mamm* this morning—hadn't finished helping Nathaniel with the morning chores yet. Thankfully, she hadn't seen him since their awkward encounter early this morning.

Was there some way she could get out of sitting down to breakfast with everyone? *Nee,* she didn't think so. *Mamm* and *Dat* would want her present. Perhaps she could go unnoticed. If she didn't say anything, *Dat* would surely carry the conversation along with Alvin Beachy. And *Mamm* would engage in conversation with Ada. And Nathaniel with Joshua. Which left her—the odd duck out. Too bad the Beachys didn't have a daughter near her age.

"What should I do with these eggs?"

Susan's head spun around so fast she nearly gave herself whiplash. She'd expected Joshua to enter the house at some point, but she hadn't expected him to sneak up behind her and give her a heart attack.

She surveyed the kitchen. Where had *Mamm* disappeared to? *Ach.*

"Clean them?" she quipped.

"Ah," The corners of his mouth lifted. "A sassy one, eh?"

She turned back to her task at hand, except...what had she been doing?

"Your *mudder* said you'd be needing more. Were you serious about wanting me to wash them? I mean, I can. You'll just need to show me where everything is."

Susan felt like snorting. "Not wash, clean." She pointed to the sink. "The sink is right there."

"Okay. Soap?"

"We don't use soap."

He looked down at the eggs in the basket, then at Susan. She chuckled at his grimace. "You don't?"

"No. No water either."

"You're pulling my leg, right?" He laughed. He had a really nice laugh. Not that she'd noticed. Or cared.

She shook her head. "No, I'm not."

"How can you clean them without water?" His baffled look made him adorable. But she wasn't attracted to him. She wasn't in the market for a man. Hunky or not. Okay, maybe she *was* a *little* attracted to him, but it didn't matter.

She joined him at the sink and picked up a scouring pad. "If you use water or some type of cleaner, it removes the egg's natural antibacterial layer. When you remove the bloom—"

"Bloom?"

"*Jah*, that's what it's called. Anyhow, when you remove the bloom, you're encouraging bacteria to grow." She plucked an egg out of the basket, then demonstrated removing the organic debris from the egg. "See?"

"How do you know that? I'm genuinely impressed."

"My brother-in-law, Titus. He used to have all kinds of chickens and a ton of eggs at any given time."

"A chicken farmer?"

"*Nee*, not really. He's sold most of the chickens since and only has a couple dozen now."

"I see."

Susan washed her hands in the empty sink, then began to retrieve the plates from the cupboard to set the table.

"Why do you use a travel trailer for the chickens?"

"You didn't ask Nathaniel?"

"I didn't think to."

"It's simple, really. *Dat* can easily move the camper around, so the chickens aren't always in the same place. The hens are experts at preparing the ground—they till it naturally and fertilize, and they eat unwanted bugs like ticks and such. During the day, they can escape the heat by lying in the cool grass under the trailer. They have laying boxes and food and water inside, so they don't stray far. At night, the hens have a cozy place to roost, generally safe from predators."

"Interesting. I've never seen that before. Is it just this Amish community that uses trailers for their chickens?"

Susan shrugged, as she placed silverware next to each plate. "I wouldn't know. Your *brieder's* community doesn't allow for it, though."

"I've heard they've been becoming stricter lately." He frowned.

"*Jah*. The leaders think our bishop is too fast."

"Is he?"

"I don't think so. I mean, *jah*, he does make some allowances if the other leaders in the district approve. And sometimes he helps people get around the rules, if you know what I mean."

"I don't, actually." He picked up an egg, then

scrubbed it as she'd demonstrated.

"Well, my sister-in-law Kayla was *Englisch*. Our community is not too eager to allow *Englischers* to join after a bad experience in the past. So, Bontrager suggested she become Amish in a more progressive group that is accepting of seekers. She became Amish that way, then she was able to come back here and marry my brother. I'm not sure the other leaders were too happy with that, so I don't see it happening again."

"I did know something about Kayla, because she and my brother had Bailey together."

Heat rose in her cheeks. That was one thing they didn't openly speak of in their house. "Right."

"So, your father mostly works in construction?" Joshua must've sensed a need to change the subject, and Susan was thankful.

"Mostly. That and farming. The farming is more for food and fun, and construction is for money." When he finished the eggs, she cracked them into a bowl, whisked them together with milk, salt, and pepper, then dumped them into the hot frying pan.

"I hear you. It's hard to make money from farming unless you have a large operation." He leaned against the sideboard. "By the way, you look good with clothes on."

"*What*?" Her jaw slacked.

"I mean, uh, you looked good without them too and with your hair undone. It's just..." He shook his head and clamped his mouth shut.

She glared at him. Of all the nerve!

"*Ach*, I don't think that came out right. What I meant to say was—"

The door from outside whooshed open.

"Is breakfast ready, *dochder*?" *Dat* waltzed into the dining area with their company in tow, just in time to save her from more humiliation. *Dat* was in his element. He loved having company over.

Susan, not so much. She didn't mind if it was just the family, but strangers could be nerve-wracking. Like Joshua, who stood staring at her.

"Almost. Go ahead and have a seat," she suggested.

Mamm finally walked back into the kitchen. Where had she been? Susan eyed her carefully. *Mamm* smiled slightly, but she wasn't herself. Was *Mamm* coming down with something? Or had she purposely vacated the kitchen knowing Joshua Beachy would be entering with the eggs?

FIVE

Jah, breakfast had been a disaster.

It had gone great until he opened his big mouth. *You look good with clothes on?* That had to be at the top of the list of stupidest things anyone's ever said. Susan's glare confirmed it.

Joshua had chastised himself a hundred times within the last thirty minutes of cleaning the barn.

"You know, the Beachy boys have a reputation in these parts." Nathaniel glanced at him over the wall of one of the adjoining stalls.

Joshua's head snapped up. "What do you mean?"

"Well, after what happened with Josiah and Kayla. And then Jaden and Martha. Any of that ring a bell?" Nathaniel smirked.

Joshua rubbed his forehead. "I see."

"We don't need any repeat performances." That sounded like a warning.

He heard the message loud and clear. "Listen, Nathaniel. I have no intentions of—"

"I see the way you've looked at *mei schweschder*. Intentions or not, just...beware."

Ach, was he that transparent? *Jah*, he admitted that he was attracted to Susan. But the likelihood of the two of them getting together seemed to be slim to none, judging by Susan's attitude toward him. Not that he blamed her. He'd made a complete idiot of himself.

Besides that, he hadn't cleared things up with Lissa yet, so he wasn't even on the dating market. He wondered what Lissa was doing now. She was likely still at her *schweschder's* and hadn't even received his letter yet. Chances were, she'd already heard about their family leaving through the grapevine. Exactly what he hadn't wanted.

"I'm not available," Joshua said.

A sardonic chuckle burst from Nathaniel's lips. "Could've fooled me. If you're not interested, you shouldn't be leading *maedels* on. Especially, when it's one of my sisters."

And there was the warning—again. Nathaniel was definitely the overprotective type when it came to his family.

"What do you mean by *not available*, anyhow?"

Nathaniel's brow quirked.

"I had an *aldi* back in Pennsylvania."

Nathaniel stopped the pitchfork in mid-sweep and stared at him. "Had or have?"

"It's complicated." Joshua sighed. "I didn't find out we were moving until just a few days prior. Lissa was out of town at her *schweschder's* helping with a new *boppli*. I'd planned to talk to her, but I haven't been able to yet. I did leave her a letter."

His eyes narrowed. "We have no use for two-timers. If you hurt my *schweschder*—"

"Like I said, I'm not planning to pursue your sister."

"Actions speak louder than words."

Joshua's skin prickled. He got the feeling that Nathaniel didn't like him very much. "I know."

"Since you're living in our *dawdi haus*, it's probably best to avoid her."

He understood Nathaniel—really he did. But he also didn't appreciate being told what to do. He was an adult, for goodness' sake. Nathaniel made him feel like doing the opposite just to prove a point. Instead of saying something in return that he might regret, he grunted and continued the task at hand.

~

"Don't forget, you'll need to gather the strawberries. And we'll need spinach for the lasagna tonight too." *Mamm* said the words without glancing away from the dough she kneaded.

Susan groaned. Just once, she'd like to have a week or two and not have any chores to do. No meal preparation, no washing, hanging, or folding laundry, no hoeing their gigantic garden, just time to herself to do whatever she pleased.

She thought of the young women she'd seen drive by in the car, with their hair blowing in the breeze. *Jah*, she wanted that carefree life. Not one filled with toil and a growing list of never-ending chores.

A heavy breath escaped her lips. It would never happen. At least, it wouldn't unless she *made* it happen. She made a mental note to write down a list of things she'd need to do to make an *Englisch* life a reality. If she had a well-thought-out plan, maybe the seemingly impossible could become possible.

She set her thoughts aside and smiled to herself. *Jah*, she'd work in the garden now. But later, she'd scurry away to her room and forge a plan that she alone would know about.

Good thing she was wearing her ugliest dress. Dirt and sweat couldn't make it any worse. Well, maybe sweat would. But it didn't matter. It wasn't like she had anybody to impress.

Susan stepped outside, but quickly realized her kerchief would be no match for the sun. She smiled to herself, then spun around and charged back inside, up the stairs, and straight to her *bruder's* room. He had an extra old straw hat that he didn't wear anymore. It would be perfect for keeping the sunburn off her nose while she worked. She'd look ridiculous, for sure, but it wasn't as if she were going to meeting or out in public.

She fetched the garden cart and tools from Emily's shed, then made her way out to the two acres that was their garden. Fortunately, *Mamm* didn't need a ton of spinach for their supper. One large freezer bag full should do the trick. She pulled out her scissors and made quick work of gathering the spinach.

Strawberries were another thing. She'd need to walk down the rows to see which berries were ripe enough to harvest. She knelt on the garden pad, continued to move down the row, and had a bowlful in no time. The best thing about a garden was that you could eat whatever you wanted while working and not have to worry about keeping a trim figure.

"Wow. You even make a brown dress look pretty."

Susan's gaze shot up at Joshua's voice. His shadow loomed over her.

He chuckled. "At first, I thought you were Nathaniel." He pointed to the straw hat she wore. "Except, I don't suspect your *bruder* wears dresses too often?"

She smiled in spite of herself. "Not since he was a *boppli*."

"What's in the bag?" Joshua gestured to the basket beside her.

"Spinach."

He made a face.

She suppressed a laugh. "You don't like spinach?"

"Nasty bitter stuff." He shook his head with vigor. "No, thanks."

"Bitter?" She reached into the bag, pulled out a leaf, and popped it into her mouth. "Nah, not bitter at all."

His brow lowered and she handed him a leaf. "Try it."

"Nope."

She rolled her eyes. "Come on, you're not a two-year-old."

He huffed, then snatched the spinach leaf from her hand and forced himself to eat it. He cocked his head to the side.

"See? Not bitter."

He swallowed the last of it and raised a shoulder. "I guess you're right. Maybe my taste buds have changed."

"*Nee*. You probably ate the mature leaves last time or maybe a different variety. These are the baby leaves. They're not only sweet, but nutritious too. Have you ever had a spinach salad?"

His lips twisted. "I try to avoid spinach at all costs."

"Well, I'll have to make you one sometime. You'll be surprised at how yummy it is." Now, why had she gone and offered to make him food? Great, now he'd think she was interested. Which she certainly was not. Not when she planned to leave as soon as the opportunity presented itself.

He plucked a strawberry from her basket, wiped it on his shirt, then devoured it.

"Hey!"

He chuckled. "Not bad." He had the audacity to steal two more.

She moved her basket out of his reach. "What do you think you're doing? I didn't pick these so they'd disappear before I get to the house." She planted a hand on her hip.

He offered a sheepish smile. "I'll replace what I ate." He reached to the row behind them, removed a few of the red berries, and deposited them into her basket. "I already finished my chore list. Would you like some help?"

"Knock yourself out." She handed him an empty

basket. "Pick only the ripe ones."

She was grateful for his help, even if Joshua Beachy was a little annoying.

"Hey, when you're done here, do you think you can wash a load of laundry for me?"

Seriously? As if she didn't already have a gazillion things to do.

"What do I look like, your maid?" She hadn't meant to say the words aloud, but they tumbled out anyhow.

His eyes widened.

Jah, he hadn't been expecting *that* reaction. Not from what was supposed to be a proper, submissive Amish woman.

"I could wash them myself, if you'd show me how."

She wanted to laugh. "You've never washed a load of laundry before?"

"*Nee.*"

"Hmm. *Mei mamm* taught all *mei brieder* to wash clothes."

"And they're expected to do women's work?"

Susan took a deep breath and uttered a prayer for patience. She would not dump her basket of strawberries over his head. She. Would. Not.

"Having a *boppli* is women's work." *Jah*, she'd said *that* aloud too.

His cheeks reddened.

"Chores have no specific gender designation," she said.

"So, you're saying that your *bruder* washes dishes and laundry and prepares meals?"

She shrugged. "Sometimes. And I occasionally muck stalls."

"But you don't shoe horses, right?" He challenged.

She shook her head. "My *bruder* Paul does. But that's a specific trade. Most people are not farriers. Are you?"

"But it isn't women's work." He completely ignored her question.

"I suppose a woman *could be* a farrier if she wanted to." She turned up her nose.

A hearty laugh burst from his lips. "You just can't be wrong, can you?"

"I'm not wrong."

He laughed again.

"Did you actually come out here to help, or to annoy me? Because if it's the latter, you're doing a great job."

He relinquished a heavy breath, then moved to another row several feet away from her.

Ach, she hadn't meant to offend him but he was truly getting on her nerves. At least now she'd be able to finish her work in peace and get out of the hot sun.

The sooner she completed her chores, the sooner she could start on her list and plan her departure from the community.

Best to avoid Joshua Beachy altogether.

SIX

How was it that Joshua managed to offend Susan Miller *every* time he opened his mouth? He'd been having fun with her, just teasing, but she hadn't seen it as such. *Nee*, she seemed to take it as a personal attack, which he hadn't meant at all.

At first, she'd even graced him with a couple adorable smiles. How had things gone downhill so quickly? Now, she avoided him like the plague. *Ach*.

As much as he would have loved for Susan to instruct him in washing laundry, he opted to wait and ask Nathaniel or *Mamm* when they were available. Nathaniel had left this morning with his *vatter* to work on a construction project, and *Mamm* and *Daed* were looking at property with a local realtor. He was grateful to the Millers for the use of their *dawdi haus*, but he couldn't wait until they purchased their own place.

Whatever home *Mamm* and *Daed* decided to purchase would eventually become his to raise his own family in. That dream seemed so far away, considering his current circumstances. He didn't see a future with Lissa anymore, but he felt awkward about attending singings in this new district.

When he'd mentioned it to Nathaniel earlier, he'd said that he and Susan no longer attended the young folks' gatherings. The thought baffled him. Did they both plan to remain single? If not, how did they expect to meet their future spouses?

Perhaps he could talk Nathaniel into going with him the first time. He'd feel too uncomfortable attending the young folks' gathering alone. Either that, or he'd wait until Justin showed up and convince his *bruder* to join him. Of course, that wouldn't be difficult to do. Justin had always looked forward to gatherings in their Pennsylvania community.

Maybe he shouldn't write Lissa off so quickly, though. Just maybe she would agree to continue to court through letters, then if things progressed to where he developed a special affection for her, she'd move out here and they'd marry. He frowned at the thought. Why did a future with Lissa no longer appeal to him? Or, perhaps he should ask himself, why was his attraction to Lissa lacking? Was it wrong to continue a relationship because it felt comfortable? Shouldn't a marriage relationship include some level of passion?

He'd dismissed his feelings at first, believing they'd eventually come naturally, but they hadn't. And it wasn't as though he didn't think Lissa was pretty. He did. There was just something amiss and no amount of effort on his part eased the uncomfortable feeling that came when he thought about taking her as a *fraa*.

Strange as it was, he felt a spark with Susan. Just being around her for a day, even with her spirited attitude and all, drew him to her. But he shouldn't be drawn to her.

He shouldn't want to tease a smile out of her at every turn. He shouldn't want to ask her if she'd give him a chance. And he certainly shouldn't want to kiss that frown off her face. She'd probably slap him if he did.

But something in his gut told him it might be worth it?

~

Maybe Susan should consider talking to her sister-in-law, Kayla. After all, she used to be an *Englischer*. She would know a lot more about how to navigate the *Englisch* world. But if she did speak to her sister-in-law, then Kayla might be inclined to tell her *bruder* Silas. Then her *bruder* might tell their folks. Then all her plans would be foiled. *Nee*, she couldn't take that chance.

If she visited the library, perhaps she could do a little research on one of their computers. If she was going to follow through with her plan, she needed to know a few things. Like where she would stay. And how much it would cost to rent her own place. And how much money she would need to make a living.

She figured that if she moved into town, she wouldn't need a vehicle. She could simply walk where she wanted to go unless the weather was foul. She thought about possibly taking her scooter along, but it would be harder to fit in with *Englischers* if she still used a mode of transportation that only the Amish used in these parts. Maybe she could learn to ride a bicycle. It was something to consider, anyhow.

She glanced down at her growing list of things she'd need to do. Buy *Englisch* clothes. Find a place to live. Find a job. Just the sheer enormity of what she was about to do was overwhelming. But the more prepared she was, the easier the transition should be, right? She'd be plunging herself into a world of total strangers and new experiences. The thought was both terrifying and thrilling.

In order to accomplish any of it, though, she'd need to hire an *Englisch* driver to take her into Madison, and then into Versailles. She should probably make two separate trips, but she was so hungry for information that she didn't want to wait another second, let alone a whole week between trips.

She'd offer to make the grocery shopping trip for *Mamm* this week. If she did, she could go by the thrift store first and try on some *Englisch* clothes. *Ach,* who would have thought she'd be purchasing *Englisch* clothes? She'd always wondered how she would look in them. Soon, she would find out.

SEVEN

Joshua peered through the screen door, then entered the summer kitchen, where Susan and her mother now slaved over the stove. Amish families, who were fortunate enough to have a detached summer kitchen, appreciated not having to warm the entire home during the stifling summer heat. Joshua certainly appreciated it, even though the humidity was much more bearable here in Indiana.

The sweet heady scent of strawberries wafted through the air. He knew by their set up, they must be cooking jam. He couldn't wait to indulge in some when the batch was finished. He could taste it now, butter slathered on a slice of fresh warm bread and topped with jam. His mouth watered just imagining it.

"It smells wonderful *gut* in here!" He couldn't suppress his grin.

"*Denki*." *Fraa* Miller cast a quick look in his direction.

Susan kept her back to him and busied herself with stirring a large pot using one of those oversized wooden utensils.

"Would I be able to use the buggy this afternoon? I'd like to go visit my *bruder* Jaden. And maybe Josiah too, if I have time."

"I don't see why not. Do you know how to get there?"

He clasped his hands together. "I was hoping Susan could show me."

Susan gasped.

Her *mamm's* smile widened. "That's perfect. Would you mind stopping by Millers' Country Store and Bakery first to pick up a couple potpies? I know Martha would really appreciate a night off from cooking."

"Sure. We could do that." Joshua smiled.

"Susan can be ready to go in about an hour, if that suits you."

"It does. *Denki*."

"There are sandwiches on the table inside the house. Help yourself to them."

His stomach grumbled just then. "I appreciate it."

He eyed Susan, who never turned around to acknowledge him. Was it because her *mamm* was present? Had she been embarrassed that he'd asked her to go with him? The woman was a mystery indeed. One he desired to solve more than any Hardy Boys book he'd ever read.

An hour later, he and Susan sat side-by-side in the spring buggy. The older buggy horse, Chocolate, had an easy gait. The breeze felt nice as they made their way toward the store that Susan's *bruder* Silas owned.

Joshua glanced at Susan. She hadn't said a word to him since getting into the buggy. He didn't have to ask to know she wasn't happy.

Again, he felt the desire to make her smile. "Is everything okay?" She looked like she had just lost her favorite pet.

"I would have appreciated being the one to decide whether I wanted to go or not," she informed him.

Ach. So that's what it was. He'd managed to offend her yet again. Would he *ever* learn?

He dropped his head. "I didn't even think. I'm sorry."

"What's even worse is my *mamm* trying to pair us up." She wrung her hands.

He eyed her carefully. "Would that be such a bad thing?"

She gaped at him, then snapped her mouth shut.

He chuckled. "You didn't answer."

"Maybe I'm still in shock that you said such a thing."

"Is that a no?"

"Joshua Beachy, if you are wanting to court me, you have a funny way of asking."

He casually lifted his brow. "What would you say if I *did* ask?"

She stared at him now. "I'd probably tell you that I'm not in a position to court anyone at the moment."

Now he was confused. "But I thought...I was under the impression...Do you already have a beau, then?"

"*Nee.*"

"Well then..." He let his words trail off. "I don't understand."

She laughed now. "Have you never been turned down by a *maedel*?"

Jah, she was making fun of him. But at least he'd coaxed a smile from her lips.

He reciprocated the gesture. It felt good to smile with Susan. "Actually, no. I haven't." He shrugged. "Not that I've asked a ton of girls."

She motioned in front of them and to the left. "It's just up ahead. There's a parking lot in front where you can hitch up Chocolate."

Subject conveniently changed. He nodded.

She pointed to a house sitting back from the road. "My *bruder* Paul and his *fraa* Jenny live right there. Jenny runs the bakery."

"The house looks *Englisch*."

"*Jah*, it was. But *mei bruder* disconnected the electric when they bought the place."

"And they've added on, by the look of it."

She nodded. "They have quite a hatful of *kinner*, so extra bedrooms were a must."

"I remember your *bruder* Paul from when we were *kinner* and your family lived in Pennsylvania. I have more memories of Silas, though, since he and Josiah were friends back in the day."

Joshua guided the horse into Silas and Kayla's driveway, then into the small parking area in front of the store.

~

Spending time with Joshua Beachy hadn't been as bad as Susan imagined it would be. She'd been surprised at how well their conversation flowed, unlike with the young men she'd accepted buggy rides from in the past. She eyed him as he hooked up Chocolate to the hitching rail. His tanned muscled arms were exposed by his rolled-up sleeves, and she acknowledged his handsome features, but the most attractive part about him was his congeniality.

She thought about their conversation during the ride and his question about courting. If she had planned to stay in the community, she might have actually considered a relationship with Joshua. Why not? He was easy to be with and easy on the eyes, and he had the ability to coax words from her mouth, it seemed. There was something about him that resonated with her soul.

"You ready?" He smiled up at her and offered a hand.

Ach, she hadn't realized she was still sitting in the buggy. Her cheeks warmed. "I can get down myself, *denki*."

He shrugged. "Suit yourself."

She hurried down.

"Are these the windchimes Silas and Paul make?" He moved his fingers over one, causing the chime to produce sound.

"*Jah*."

"Nice. I saw the one your *bruder* made for your *mamm*. I like them." He held the door to the store open, and she walked in ahead of him.

"*Guten tag, schweschder*," a male voice greeted from behind the counter.

"Silas?" Susan frowned. "What are you doing in here? Does Kayla have you making pies?"

Silas chuckled and glanced down at himself. "You like my apron?"

Joshua held out his hand to Silas. "Nice to see you, Silas."

Silas's expression expanded. "Josh Beachy, right?"

Joshua nodded.

"Wow, the last time I saw you you were just a little guy."

"I know. Justin and I never made it out for any of the weddings. We had to hold down the fort at home."

"And you weren't home when I went to Pennsylvania with Josiah," Silas said.

"*Nee*. Justin and I were out of town. It was just Jaden then. This is actually my first time in Indiana."

"Is it really? Well, welcome to the Hoosier state."

"*Denki*."

Silas rubbed his hands together. "Is there something I can get for you?"

Susan looked behind her oldest bruder. "Are you here alone?"

"No. You think Jenny and Kayla would trust me here by myself?" He laughed. "Bailey's here. She ran up to the house to make sure Shiloh has everything under control. The ladies have a well-deserved day off, so they went shopping."

As though she'd heard her name, Bailey waltzed

through the back double doors and into the baking area. A huge smile spread across her face as she rounded the corner and engulfed Joshua in an embrace. "*Onkel* Josh! I didn't expect to see you in here today."

Bailey's gaze moved from Susan to Joshua, then back again.

"*Mamm* sent us over to pick up some potpies to take to Jaden and Martha's," Susan explained.

"I heard you're married and have a *boppli* now." Joshua smiled at his niece.

"Yep, you'll meet Timothy at church if we don't stop by sooner. But I'm thinking we will, because I know *Dawdi* Alvin and *Mammi* Ada are aching to see the *boppli*."

"I'm sure and certain they'll like that," Joshua agreed. "Best come by in the evening, though, because they've been going out during the daytime looking at properties."

"What about the house across the street from *Mammi* and *Dawdi* Millers' place?"

"They've looked at that, but they prefer more property. Might have to settle for less if they can't find what they want." Joshua shrugged.

"They're staying in the *dawdi haus*, so you can imagine how cramped they'll be when Justin shows up," Susan said.

"Ah, it's fine for now. We're grateful to have any place."

Silas spoke up. "How many of those potpies did you need? I reckon you two better get a move on if you're going all the way to Detweiler's district. It's quite a drive by buggy. At this rate, you probably won't be home till dark."

"Two should be enough," Susan said.

~

An hour later, Joshua and Susan were enjoying time with their niece and nephew in Martha's living room.

"They're just so cute, aren't they?" Joshua tickled Nelson's tummy.

"Just wait until you have your own, *bruder*." Jaden grinned. "It does something funny to your insides. I feel like I'd do anything for the babies or Martha."

"Someday, maybe." Joshua briefly lifted his eyes and for a split second met Susan's.

Susan didn't miss Martha's intake of breath. Her *schweschder* immediately grabbed her hand and led her to the kitchen, out of earshot of the men.

"Alright, *schweschder*. *What* was *that* all about?" Martha demanded in a semi-whisper. *Ach*, she'd seen Joshua's look too? *Oh, dear*.

"I don't know what you mean." Susan feigned

innocence and pretended to be distracted by the baby in her arms.

"Don't you even. I know when something's going on."

Right. Her *schweschder* could sniff out a juicy piece of gossip a mile away.

"Nothing is going on. Trust me."

Martha shook her head. "Joshua Beachy likes you. That's plain to see."

"So?"

"Don't tell me you don't find him attractive." Martha pointed at her. "I watched your banter on the way in. There's something there."

Susan sighed. Oh boy. How was she going to change her older sister's mind? "There is nothing, really. We're just friends."

"Well, *just friends* is a great place to start. Jaden and I were just friends before we started courting."

"It's not the same as you and Jaden."

"It could be, by the look on Josh's face."

"Stop, Martha. Nothing will become of Joshua and me."

"You don't know that."

"*Jah*, I do." Because she wouldn't let it. She was moving away from the community. Of course, she couldn't share that with her *schweschder*. She'd never hear the end of it.

The little one in Susan's arms squealed as she played with the ribbon on her prayer *kapp*. She would miss these little ones once she was gone. Come to think of it, she'd miss everyone. Even Joshua Beachy.

EIGHT

Joshua jostled the reins as they headed back toward the Millers' place. Truth be told, he enjoyed spending time with Susan. He enjoyed her feistiness, but she was even more fun when she let her guard down and wasn't trying to prove anything. He'd seen how she was with the *bopplin,* and how she'd helped with changing their diapers and feeding them. She would make a *gut mamm.* He was convinced of it.

He cleared his throat. "Earlier, on the way to your *bruder's* store, you'd said you weren't in a position to date anyone. What does that mean exactly? Are you waiting for someone? Are you already seeing somebody?"

"*Nee.*"

"Then why?"

"I have my reasons." She clasped her hands in her lap and looked away.

He reached over and covered her hands with one of his. "Will you tell me why?"

"I can't."

"I don't understand." He eyed her. "If you have something to say, you can share it with me. I won't tell. Promise." He held up two fingers.

She blew out a breath and glanced at him, her expression communicating doubt.

"You can trust me, Susan. Seriously. I feel like we've become friends."

"*Ach*, it would be nice to share my dreams with someone. But I don't..." She pressed her lips together. "Do you ever feel like you want more out of life?"

"Like what?"

Her shoulders rose and fell. "I'm not exactly sure. I just feel like there is so much out there and I'm missing out on it."

"Didn't you go on a mission trip in another country?"

She nodded. "Central America."

"And what did you think? Did you enjoy being away?"

"Very much. I mean, I felt sorry for the people there, and I think it made me grateful for what I have. But still, I just want to experience things outside of our community. Not anywhere far away, but just around here. I want to be free to live as I please."

"What do you want to experience?"

"Oh, I don't know exactly. Maybe driving a car. Living on my own apart from the Amish community."

He leaned back, eyes wide. "Really? You'd want to leave your family and community? Become *Englisch*?"

She dipped her head, then stared at him. "You said you wouldn't tell."

"I won't, but..." His jaw dropped and disappointment filled his entire being. He rubbed his forehead. "So, you would leave and marry amongst the *Englisch*?"

She shrugged. "I don't know. I haven't thought that far, really. Right now, I just can't see myself married at all. To anyone."

The sadness that overtook him was indescribable. Couldn't she see all the blessings around her? Couldn't she see how she was protected here in the community? Couldn't she see that he'd begun to develop feelings for her?

If only he could pull the buggy off on one of the side roads and show Susan how wonderful a kiss could be. If she knew he was beginning to care for her, would it make a difference? Would it change her mind? *Nee*, he thought not. But he knew he had to try.

"I see." He swallowed. Now he understood why she'd said she wasn't in a position to date. But something urged him to do his best to change her mind. She was Amish. She belonged here with their people, not out in the strange and unfamiliar *Englisch* world.

Joshua thought of his *bruder* Josiah. He'd lived in the *Englisch* world for a good portion of his life. Yet, here he was, living amongst their people again. Would Susan do the same thing? Or would she find all that she was looking for out in the *Englisch* world?

Another question Joshua didn't want to ponder was, would he be willing to wait for Susan? If so, for how long?

His *bruder* had lost out on a relationship with his first *dochder's mamm*. Would Susan lose out on a *gut* Amish man?

"I don't want to go back yet. Do you?" he said.

Susan shrugged. "It doesn't really matter."

Gut. "Is there a park or someplace similar around here?"

Her eyes lit up. "There's a small one across from the library. But it's a little bit of a drive."

He smiled. "I don't mind if you don't. I'd like to see your library."

"It's your library now, too." She smiled again. "I

64

was hoping to go there. But we'll need to hurry. They will close in an hour."

~

Susan smiled to herself as she and Joshua traveled toward home. Maybe her leap into the *Englisch* world was closer than she'd thought! She could almost kiss Joshua Beachy for taking her to the library.

While he had been checking out the library, she'd cornered a librarian to ask about finding a place to rent. The young woman suggested looking in the local newspaper. Susan had found one listing and took down the phone number. She'd call later for details. Unfortunately, the listing didn't mention a price, so she had no idea what to expect to pay.

She had a little bit of money saved up from when she and Martha had cleaned houses for *Englischers*. Hopefully, it could get her something until she could find a job to support herself.

She'd thought of little else since they'd begun their final journey home.

"Would you mind showing me around the property when we get back?" Joshua eyed her. It seemed his mind had been lost in contemplation as well.

"You could ask Nathaniel." Because people might get the wrong idea if the two of them were to disappear together.

He grimaced. "I don't think your *bruder* likes me all that much."

Susan laughed. "That's not surprising. He tends to be overprotective."

"I gathered that. Truth be told, I feel more comfortable with you."

"Well, I'm sure supper will be on the table when we get back."

"*Gut.* Because I'm hungry. Although, those potpies were delicious."

"*Jah.* Kayla has a reputation around here. Everyone loves her potpies."

"Well, I can see why." He raised a brow. "After supper, then?"

"If you help with dishes." Susan smiled.

"Done."

~

Joshua admitted he had ulterior motives in asking Susan to show him the Miller property. He *had to* change her mind about going into the *Englisch* world. Although, he wasn't sure how to go about it. He'd been praying *Der Herr* would grant him wisdom in this matter, but so far his prayers had seemed to fall on deaf ears.

He hadn't realized that by taking her to the library, he'd been fueling her quest to leave. It wasn't until he'd overheard Susan speaking with the librarian—*jah*, he admitted he'd been eavesdropping—about finding a place to rent, that he'd realized his dreadful mistake. Not that she wouldn't have eventually been seeking it out on her own. He just didn't have any desire to hasten her departure.

"The pond is just down by the woods." Susan led the way.

He glanced back to see if Nathaniel still had his eagle eye trained on them. If Joshua couldn't get her alone, he wouldn't be able to convince her to stay. Really, he had no desire to see the pond or the rest of the property. "Is this where the property ends?"

She laughed. "Oh, goodness, no. It ends at the creek."

"I hadn't realized there was a creek too. Where is it?"

She pointed ahead of them. "In the woods."

"Is there a path to it?"

"*Jah.*"

He couldn't help but smile. This would be perfect. Or, he hoped it would. "Will you show me?"

"Sure." She continued and he hurried to catch up with her. "Let me walk with you just in case there are snakes or anything."

"Have you ever encountered a snake?" Her glance shot in his direction.

"Many times." He bent down and picked up a broken branch. "I usually just move it out of the way with something like this or wait until it passes by. It's best not to disturb them if you can help it."

She shuttered. "I hate snakes."

He chuckled. "Well, I'm not particularly fond of them either. But I suppose they have their purpose."

"If their purpose is scaring me, they do a good job."

"You don't need to be afraid." In a bold move, he reached for her hand and squeezed it. He would have held it longer, but he didn't know how she'd respond. "They'll usually leave you alone if they don't feel threatened."

"Can we talk about something else?" She shivered. "This isn't my favorite subject."

Right. *Real smooth, Sherlock.*

"So, does anyone know about your plans to leave?"

She frowned and stared at him, wide-eyed. "My plans?"

"Susan, I know you weren't just talking about dreams. I see the determination in your eyes. You have plans."

"You said you wouldn't tell."

He knew they were almost to the creek when he heard the gentle flow of water tumbling over rocks. "And I won't. But you've got to know that your family is going to worry about you."

"I plan to leave them a note." She stopped at the water's edge. "And there's no need for them to worry. I'll be fine."

He stood next to her, but it was difficult to appreciate the beauty around them when his heart ached so.

He turned to look at her. "I'll miss you."

Her eyes finally came to rest on his. Indecision seemed to war within their depths.

He dared to lift his hand to her cheek. "I'll worry about you too." His thumb moved to the side of her mouth, and he felt her tremble under his touch.

"I..." She opened her mouth, but the words seemed to flee. She must've felt the magnetic pull between them too.

"Susan, I..." He could no longer resist the urge to drop his lips to hers. When she didn't protest but responded in kind, he took that as an invitation. His hand moved behind her head and his mouth captured hers, tasting the cinnamon that must've been in the apple pie they'd enjoyed for dessert. Her kiss was nothing short of heavenly.

Ach, this was something he'd hoped to feel with Lissa but never had. *Lissa*. The one he still hadn't officially broken up with. Although he'd had every intention of doing so.

He reluctantly broke contact but stared down at her obviously-been-kissed lips. Lissa or no, he desired more. And by the look of it, Susan did too. He coaxed her close once again and delighted when her fingers feathered through his hair at the nape of his neck. His mouth moved slowly to taste her jawline, her neck. He wanted to savor every blissful second. "Susan." He caught his breath. "You're what I've been missing. Everything I want."

At his words, she pushed away. "No."

"Why?"

"You know why. I'm not staying." Tears now shimmered in her eyes.

He took her hand. "Please give us a chance. Stay." He hadn't expected his voice to crack.

His heart had ached before at the thought of her leaving, but now? *Ach*, now it was a hundred times worse. Now the hope of a future with Susan had been birthed in his heart.

"Don't do this, Joshua. You know I can't stay." A tear trickled down her cheek.

"But you *can*. Don't you see?" He brushed her tears away, forbidding his own.

"*Nee*, I can't!" She spun around and charged toward the house like she was being chased by a swarm of wasps.

With all his heart, he wanted to follow after her. But somehow he knew it would be pointless. Maybe after she had time to contemplate the situation, she'd change her mind. *Jah*, he'd pray for that.

NINE

If only Joshua Beachy wasn't the most wonderful man she'd ever met. Because, if he wasn't, her decision to escape would be simple. Easy, even.

But Joshua...

She couldn't get his gentle ways—or his amazing kisses—out of her head. She couldn't forget the sincerity in his gaze. Neither could she forget his heartfelt pleas.

What would it be like if she gave him—them—a chance? Would her desire for the *Englisch* world fade away? She knew it would not.

If they began a courting relationship, she was certain it would end in marriage. Because that was how fantastic Joshua Beachy was. He'd caused something deep inside of her come alive. But she knew she wasn't ready for that yet. She'd been selfish to allow him to kiss her, to lead him on and give him hope that there could be more between them. But in all fairness, he knew where she stood before initiating the kiss. *Nee*, kisses.

Ach, they had been the most wonderful kisses she'd ever received. Hands down. And, truth be told, she probably wouldn't resist if he initiated another one, God help her.

Joshua Beachy was truly one of a kind. The best kind.

Which was exactly why she had to nix the idea of a future with him.

~

As soon as breakfast was finished and dishes were done, Susan informed *Mamm* she'd called their usual driver last night and arranged a ride into town to go to the grocery store.

"Oh good. We were starting to run out of some things." *Mamm* handed her money from the cookie jar she kept grocery money in, along with a list.

"I was thinking of dropping by the thrift store too. Do you need anything?" Susan smiled.

"Now that I think about it, could you see if they have another stock pot like the one we have? Only get it if it has a lid, though." *Mamm's* finger flew into the air. "And look for any other gadgets that might come in handy."

Susan grinned as she added *Mamm's* request to the list. "I thought you didn't like a lot of gadgets."

"It depends on what it is." *Mamm's* brow furrowed. "Oh, and look in the craft section too. Sometimes I find great deals there. I could use more blank cards if they have them."

"Blank cards." She wrote it down. *Mamm* always liked to make her own greeting cards. Many in their community did. "Okay, well if there's anything else, you can always call the driver."

"I hate to do that."

"Well, it's better than an extra trip into town."

"You're right." *Mamm* surveyed the empty house. "Whatever am I going to do here all by myself? The house is getting quieter with each one that leaves."

Joshua had gone with *Dat* and Nathaniel to the construction site today, and his folks planned to look at another house that the realtor had informed them had just hit the market, then they'd planned to go visit Josiah's family.

"Enjoy some time alone. Read a book. Get off your feet. Relax." Because after Susan left for *gut, Mamm* would bear more of the household burdens. Guilt threatened to talk her out of her plans, but she quickly dismissed it. "You'll have no one to make lunch for but yourself. I should be back in plenty of time to help with supper."

"Get some ice cream, too. It'll be a treat, ain't not?"

"I'm sure everyone will like it. The usual?" Susan put ice cream on the list.

"*Nee*. Get a few different kinds. That chocolate one your *dat* likes, maybe fruit, and something else? You'll figure it out."

"I could get vanilla to go with the pie." Just then, Susan heard a vehicle pull up outside. "She's here. I'd better go."

~

A half hour later, Susan nervously moved through the women's clothing in the thrift store. She hoped she wouldn't see anyone she knew. As it was, the driver had come into the store too, but she was on the opposite side.

If Susan quickly picked out a few things and paid for them, she could conceal them in a bag. But she had no idea what sizes she wore, and the try-on rooms weren't open today. Was she supposed to hide in the corner and pull the jeans up under her dress to see if they fit? *Nee*, that would be quite embarrassing if someone happened upon her while she tried them on. And then what if someone thought she was trying to steal them? *Ach*, that would be a nightmare! Instead, she just held each item up to herself. Hopefully, that would work.

She chose two pairs of jeans in different sizes, a skirt, and three tops. Her cheeks heated just thinking of herself in these. *Mamm* would never approve.

To attempt to cover the items she'd added to her cart, she found a large jacket *Dat* or Nathaniel could wear. Relief flooded her when her driver motioned that she'd be waiting in the car. She needed to quickly look for the things *Mamm* requested, then leave the store as soon as possible. If she added a couple of books for the family, they could help hide the other contents too.

~

Once she arrived at home, a few hours later, she quickly summoned *Mamm* to the car to help with groceries. When *Mamm* was outside, she smuggled the forbidden clothing items up to her bedroom and tucked them away under her bed. She'd try them on later.

~

Susan peeked out the window of the phone shanty, her fingers trembling as she dialed the number to the apartment ads. She'd stolen away as soon as she finished helping with supper preparations. The casserole was now baking in the summer kitchen, so she had a little while before she needed to head back to the house. The men would return from work any time now, so she should complete her calls as quickly as possible.

"Quiet View Apartments, may I help you?"

"Yes. I saw your ad in the paper. I wanted to know how much rent costs?"

"We lease out the units yearly and require two months' rent down, along with a cleaning deposit." The man told her the amount she'd need to move in, and it stole her breath away. "You don't rent by the month?"

"Nah, nobody does that around here."

"*Ach*, I cannot afford that much."

"Sorry, ma'am."

"Do you know of any rooms for rent?" It would be awkward sharing a house with strangers, but it might be her only option. *Ach*, this wasn't turning out how she'd imagined it would.

"You know, I heard the guy at the motel sometimes rents out his units. Not sure if he has anything available. You might want to try there."

"The motel?" She frowned. That didn't sound right. She remembered the few times her family had vacationed. If she remembered correctly, her father had paid at least a hundred dollars for each night. She couldn't afford a hundred dollars a night. Even if it was half that amount, she wouldn't be able to afford it. "Uh, okay. Thank you."

She heaved a sigh and hung up the phone. How was she to leave if she couldn't find a place to live?

TEN

Joshua's day had been long and tiring but rewarding as well. Since he'd only ever worked on the farm with *Daed*, he was by no means an expert in construction. He'd been the brunt of many good-natured jokes today, but he hadn't minded. A person couldn't know every aspect of every field of expertise, could he?

He'd been grateful to learn some of the ins and outs of building a house from the ground up. Not that he would ever say that he'd learned it all. *Nee*, it would likely take decades to accumulate all the knowledge Nathaniel's father had. The man was brilliant, and so very patient.

Unlike Nathaniel.

Of course, he suspected that Nathaniel's aggravation stemmed from Joshua's spending time with his *schweschder*—*after* Nathaniel had specifically warned him not to. Joshua wasn't about to allow anyone, let alone someone years younger than him, dictate his life choices for him. That just wasn't going to happen. The *Ordnung* was strict enough without piling extra rules on top of it.

Now that they were back at the Millers' place, he looked forward to a good hearty meal and a relaxing evening. And seeking out an opportunity to spend time alone with Susan. *If* he could talk her into it. He'd thought of her, and the kisses they'd shared, several times throughout the day. It had brought many a silly smile to his face. He hadn't realized it until he began receiving funny looks from his coworkers. A construction site was not the best place to do your daydreaming, he'd quickly learned.

Oh, but if only Susan would give their relationship a chance to blossom. They made a *gut* team. He'd noticed that while out picking berries with her. It had been different with Lissa. Since she'd always spent her time in her father's temperature-controlled furniture store, work out-of-doors never appealed much to her. Not that there was anything wrong with working inside. It was just that Joshua planned to be a farmer, a job he loved. If he had a *fraa* who enjoyed it too, he'd consider it a blessing from the Lord. Of course, he wouldn't expect her to be out with him *all* the time.

There were still plenty of indoor tasks that the women in their community usually did, like food preparation and laundry and tending to young *bopplin*.

But besides all that, he and Susan had a camaraderie. Conversation was easy with Susan, and they'd even teased each other a time or two. He could certainly envision a future with her as his *fraa*. Someday. *Gott* willing.

But that vision would likely never come to fruition if she was leaving their people.

Nathaniel walked into the house, just as *Mamm* and the Miller women were putting food on the table. He handed an envelope to Joshua, and his brow shot up. "A letter from your *aldi*?"

At the words, Susan's gaze narrowed in on him and her questioning stare pierced him. He wanted to deny the words, but it would be a lie.

"A letter came from Lissa?" Judging by their looks, *Mamm's* excitement wasn't missed by anyone in the room, including Susan.

He'd planned to ignore Nathaniel, but he couldn't ignore *Mamm*, no matter who was present.

"*Jah*."

"Oh, *gut*. Do you suppose she received your letter yet?"

Ach, he really didn't want to have this conversation

in front of everybody—especially not Susan. His hapless gaze flickered to her, then he addressed his mother. "*Nee*, I doubt it. She'd planned to stay at her *schweschder's* for at least two weeks. It's barely been over one. It wonders me how she got this address."

"*Dat* left it with your *bruder*." As if that explained everything. It didn't.

"So, she likely knows we're in Indiana by now." Joshua frowned. "I'll have to call Justin later."

"You could call Lissa too if she left a phone number," *Mamm* suggested.

Jah, she likely had. Joshua swallowed and nodded.

If only *Mamm* would've waited to have this conversation at another time, in another place. But she had no idea that he had his sights set on Susan. *Nee*, for all *Mamm* knew, he and Lissa were still an item. She'd probably assumed they were still courting via letters.

"Should we eat?" Joshua could hug *Fraa* Miller for interrupting the conversation. If only she'd done it sooner. Before Susan had determined he was a two-timing jerk, and he'd likely ruined any chance of swaying her decision to stay in the community.

Susan whispered something to her *Mamm*, then rushed out of the room. But not before Joshua got a glimpse of the betrayed look in her eyes.

Her father called out to her. "Susan—"

His words halted when his *fraa* touched his arm. "She's not hungry. Let her be." A silent communication passed between the two of them.

Susan's footsteps on the stairs reminded Joshua of what a *dummkopp* he was. And that his fantasy earlier in the day would remain just that.

Ach, how he wanted to rush after her and tell her... *Tell her what?* That, *jah*, Lissa was technically still his *aldi*. Because, like it or not, that was the truth of the matter. As far as Lissa knew, their relationship was set in stone. Unless she'd received his letter.

He'd have to do damage control later when Susan could stand to look at him again. If that ever happened.

~

Susan wiped away a tear.

So much for Joshua Beachy being the perfect man.

He already had an *aldi*? If that was the case, then why in the world had he kissed her? Why had he given her false hope? Why had he set her heart in motion, causing her to believe that they might have a future together? Someday.

If he'd denied the accusations, she might think she'd been mistaken—that Nathaniel had been mistaken. But Joshua hadn't denied it. And his conversation with his mother just proved it further.

What did he think? That he could have two *aldis*—one in Pennsylvania and one here in Indiana?

If there was anything she couldn't stand, Joshua Beachy's kind was it. Cheaters. She had no use for them whatsoever. No matter how handsome they were. No matter how genuine they claimed to be. No matter how *wunderbaar* their kisses were. Because every single word of affection had been a bold-faced lie.

How dare he.

This poor Lissa person probably had no idea that her beau was a jerk, either. He'd been away from her—what—all a week? Maybe. And here he was jumping into a physical relationship with another woman! The nerve.

Honestly, she was better off without Joshua Beachy.

It would be best if she left sooner rather than later. She'd call a driver at the first opportunity she got. Perhaps someone could even pick her up this evening.

She'd slip out to the phone shanty, then scribble a note and leave it in her room. While she waited for the driver, she'd try her *Englisch* clothes on and pack a small bag that she would drop from her window and

86

smuggle out to the vehicle unnoticed. Hopefully.

Nee, she hadn't found a place to stay yet. But she would figure it out. Because, at this point in time, there was no other option.

Her heart couldn't bear to see Joshua Beachy's guilty face—and his betrayal—again.

ELEVEN

Susan never did summon the courage to ask the driver for a recommendation for a place to stay. If she had, word would likely have gotten back to her folks. Instead, she'd asked to be dropped off at one of the local fast-food restaurants. No driver would think of the request as odd. She'd figure out a place to stay from there.

Except, it was near closing and she still had nothing to go on.

On the way to the fast-food place, though, they had passed a little motel. Was that the one the man on the phone had referred to? Were there even any other motels in this tiny town? Not that she knew of. Of course, she'd never had need to seek one out.

Fortunately, the motel was within walking distance. After divesting herself of her Amish dress and prayer *kapp* in the fast-food restaurant's restroom, she set off on foot. One good thing about small towns was that everything was generally close together. No need for a car or horse and buggy.

Although she didn't have high hopes for the motel, desperation compelled her onward. She found a little building with a sign that said OFFICE, but the door had been locked. A sign on the door listed a phone number to call after hours. Where could she find a phone? Did any public payphones still exist?

She quickly jotted down the number and slipped it into the pocket of her jeans. She glanced down at her outfit and thought about her prayer *kapp*. It was surely crushed in her backpack now. She thought of all the time she'd spent ironing the thing to get it just right so she wouldn't be called out on it by one of the leaders. It was actually a bit of relief not having to worry about that anymore. It was freeing to think that she could walk around town with her head uncovered and no one would think twice about it.

Now she blended in with everybody else. At least, she hoped she did. She may look like an *Englischer*, but she certainly didn't feel like one.

Susan hiked her backpack over her shoulder. Would people think it was odd for a young woman to be trekking down the street at this hour of the night? It didn't matter. What did matter was that she locate a telephone. Determined, she continued walking toward where she thought there might be one. Had she seen one near the IGA? One of the other stores or restaurants? She couldn't remember. But she had to try.

"May I help you?"

The male voice caused Susan to jump. She hadn't even noticed the police car that had pulled up next to her.

"Sorry if I frightened you."

She shook her head. "No, it's okay. I guess I must have been daydreaming." *Ach*, but she'd never spoken to a police officer before. All of a sudden, anxiety took ahold of her. Had she been doing something wrong?

"Do you need any help?" the officer asked again.

"Um...no. Thank you." She shook her head, attempting to gather her incoherent thoughts. "Unless... do you know where there might be a payphone?"

He frowned. "A payphone?" His lips twisted. "There used to be a couple, but I'm not sure if they're still there or even working anymore."

Her hope deflated. *No payphones?*

"You don't have a cell phone?"

"No."

He shrugged. "Well, I don't usually do this, especially on duty, but I can let you use mine." He pulled his phone from his pocket and handed it to her.

Relief flooded through her. "Really? Thank you so much."

She accepted the phone, hoping her face communicated the gratefulness she felt.

"Just so long as you're not calling to China or anything. Unless it's China, Indiana."

"I don't know anybody in China."

She ignored his amused look. Did he think it odd that she didn't know anyone in China? Why would he even assume she would want to call China in the first place?

"It was supposed to be a joke. Epic fail." He murmured the last words.

She humored him by nodding, because she was too nervous to do anything else, then pulled the slip of paper from her pocket, feeling a bit awkward standing on the side of the road next to a police car. Would people suspect she was a bad person?

She dialed the phone number and waited until someone answered. "Hello." Susan spoke into the phone. "Do you have any empty rooms available to rent?"

"I'm sorry, we only have nightly rooms available right now," a male voice answered.

Oh no. "Oh. How much is it for one night?"

The man told her the amount.

Tears pricked her eyes. It wasn't as much as her father had paid when the family had gone out of town, but it was more than she could afford if she hoped to have enough money for rent. Her funds would disappear too quickly if she paid nightly.

"Miss, are you interested?" The voice echoed through the phone.

"No. I'm sorry. I'm looking for a place to rent."

"Wish I could help you out, but..."

"I understand. Thank you." She pushed the button to end the call and blinked back the tears that threatened. She handed the phone to the officer.

"Did you find what you need?"

"No, not really. I was looking for a place to rent."

The officer frowned. "What are you going to do?"

"I haven't figured that out yet."

"Well, if you're out of options, I could give you a ride to the Hart House. It's a temporary shelter for folks who have been displaced."

"Where is it? Is it within walking distance?"

"Oh no. It's several miles down the 50, between Dillsboro and Aurora."

She shook her head. "I was really hoping to find a place of my own. In Versailles. I don't have a vehicle."

"May I see your ID, miss?"

"Did I do something wrong? Am I in trouble?"

"Not that I know of. But we can't have you roaming the streets all hours of the night. It isn't safe." He held out his hand, palm up. "Your ID, please?"

Ach, he must suspect her of something. "I don't have any ID."

"How old are you?"

"I'm of age, if that's what you're concerned about."

"But you have no ID?"

Ach, why did this man have to be so intrusive?

"I come from the Amish."

"Ah, now I see. Did you just leave, then?"

"I'd rather not talk about it."

His eyes widened. "Are you in danger? Were you?"

"No, not at all." Well, maybe in danger of losing her heart. "I just wanted to live on my own."

He tapped his hands on the steering wheel. "I'm concerned about you, miss. Where will you sleep tonight?"

"Do you have any ideas? Know of any place I could rent?"

"During daytime hours, perhaps we could find you something." He grimaced, then held up a finger. "Give me a minute, please."

She nodded and he rolled up his window. It looked like he might be on the phone. Hopefully, he wasn't calling in another cop. *Ach*, how did she get herself in to this predicament?

The window of the patrol car rolled down. "Miss, will you step inside the car, please?"

Her heart thudded against her chest. "Do I have to?"

"You're not in trouble, miss."

Then why...

"It's easier to talk if you're sitting next to me. Besides, it looks like it's getting a little chilly out there."

She hesitated, then began opening the back door.

"The front's fine, miss."

Ach, she'd never been inside of a police car. She opened the door, willing her heart to slow its beat. She stuffed her shaky hands under her legs.

"Are you okay?"

"I'm nervous." She stared at all the fancy gadgets. She never knew police cars had computers inside them.

"I noticed. I promise I won't bite." A small smile formed at the corner of his mouth, and their eyes connected for the first time.

It was then that she recognized him as another human being and not just as a police officer. She admitted this young man was handsome, but he didn't compare to Joshua Beachy.

Ach, she *had to* stop thinking about Joshua. Not only was he already taken, but he was a two-timing cheat. A thief of hearts. She didn't need somebody who might leave her for another woman in the future. Joshua Beachy was clearly *not* relationship material. That was, *if* she was looking for a relationship. Which she wasn't. She needed to keep reminding herself of that. She *should have* reminded herself of that *before* she'd allowed him to kiss her. No doubt, he'd shared the same kind of kisses with his *aldi*. And if he had the same infamous Beachy blood running through his veins as his brothers, maybe he'd shared even more. Had he just been looking for a *gut* time? A fling?

She frowned at the horrifying thought. *Nee*, Joshua Beachy could not be trusted. Not with her heart or anything else. Which made her worry now. He had been the only one she'd confided in about leaving. He'd felt safe at the time, somehow. *Ach*, she'd been a fool for trusting him. Surely, he'd tell someone. Wouldn't he?

"I might have a solution for you." The officer tapped the dash, bringing her thoughts to the present. "I just got off the phone with my mom."

Her forehead wrinkled. "Your mom?"

He nodded. "I just started my shift. Won't be off till morning. My family has had pretty good relationships with the Amish, otherwise I wouldn't be offering this."

"I don't understand."

"My bedroom will be vacant tonight, so you're welcome to use it. I just called my mom and she said she wouldn't mind. And she'd make you breakfast in the morning." He held up a hand. "I know it's not an ideal situation, but you seem to be stuck between a rock and a hard place. It's either my mom's or the Hart House. Your choice."

Gratefulness filled her heart. "Your mother would let me stay in her house?"

"Yes."

"But you're a police officer."

He laughed now. "I know. This is totally unconventional. But I promise you that I'm a real person too, not just a police officer." He was teasing her. "I'd feel much better if you were off the streets. So, how about it?"

"You really don't mind?"

"No. And our house is within walking distance. Just a few houses down that street, actually." He pointed in front of them.

It would feel weird to sleep in a stranger's house, but it would be better than sleeping out on the street.

She nodded. "Thank you."

TWELVE

*J*oshua tossed and turned all night, but sleep hadn't come. The sound of activity in the kitchen compelled him to investigate. Perhaps he could find Susan alone and they could talk.

"*Guten Morgen*, Joshua. Would you mind fetching Susan for me?" Susan's *mamm* asked.

"Me?" He squeaked out.

"Top of the stairs, first door on the left," she instructed.

He nodded in uncertainty, unsure whether his face was the first one Susan wanted to see this morning, then made his way up the stairs.

"What are you doing up here?" Nathaniel's rough tone from behind, along with his rigid stance and accusing gaze, had startled him.

His hand paused on the doorknob. "Your *mamm* asked me to get Susan."

"I'll get her. Go back downstairs."

Joshua hated giving in to Nathaniel's wishes, but after what happened yesterday, he wasn't about to argue. He began descending the stairs when he heard Nathaniel's voice.

"*Mamm*, you have to see this." Nathaniel shoved past him, flew down the stairs, and rushed to the kitchen.

Confused, Joshua glanced toward Susan's open door, then hurried downstairs to see what had Nathaniel in a tizzy.

Nathaniel held a sheet of lined paper in his hand, while his mother silently read the words. His icy stare pierced Joshua's heart.

"What is it?" Joshua asked.

"She left, that's what. Susan's gone." Fury simmered in Nathaniel's eyes.

"Gone?"

"What did you expect?" Nathaniel charged toward him and grasped a fistful of his shirt. "This is all your fault. I told you to stay away from her."

"Nathaniel, *nee*!" his mother said.

He ignored his mother, violating Joshua's personal space. "The last thing we need is another—"

"Nathaniel!" It was his father's voice this time. "This is not our way."

Nathaniel reluctantly released his grip, but his fury was palpable.

"Susan's gone, *Dat*. She's left to the *Englisch* world and it's all because of him." Nathaniel's finger pointed at Joshua's chest.

"Even if that is the case, Joshua Beachy is a guest in this house. You will treat him with respect," his father demanded.

As much as Joshua wanted to argue and defend himself, he wouldn't. To his knowledge, he was the only one who knew of Susan's desire to leave. He'd promised Susan that he wouldn't tell of her plans, and he intended to keep that promise. Maybe that was one thing he could actually do right.

Ach, he'd made such a disaster of things.

He was torn between a desire to seek her out and find her, or to let her be. He knew he wouldn't be able to convince her against her will. Clearly, she'd *wanted* to leave.

But that had been *before* their kisses. Perhaps, given more time, she would have changed her mind and decided to stay.

Then he'd gone and blown it. *Ach*, he should have told her about Lissa up front when they were talking about courtship on their excursion to Jaden and Martha's. Would it have made a difference to Susan if she'd known he'd left Lissa a note basically ending their relationship? Or would she think he was insensitive?

He wasn't trying to be. He still desired to have a conversation with Lissa and explain things from his point of view. She deserved to hear the truth straight from his mouth.

Maybe he should have attempted to go see her at her sister's place. Maybe he should have made more of an effort. Maybe the reason he hadn't was because Lissa didn't have the same effect on him that Susan had.

She'd never had a hold on his heart. If she had, he would have stayed in Pennsylvania. Somehow, he'd known she wasn't the one for him. Even though he had no idea the one for him was right here in Indiana.

Ach, Susan.

The truth was, he was worried about her. Where would she be have spent the night? Did she have *Englisch* contacts, other than drivers? Was she safe?

She was smart, so he knew she likely had a plan. Nevertheless, he felt compelled to find her. He needed to see her to ensure everything was all right. Because, if anything bad happened to her...

Nee, he wouldn't let it.

THIRTEEN

Susan was surprised when a knock on the door awakened her. *Ach*, she usually woke up without Nathaniel or *Mamm* knocking on her door. She must have slept in later than usual. She yawned and shot up, her bare feet swinging around to the floor. Her eyes fully opened when she felt carpet under her feet instead of hardwood.

That was when she remembered she wasn't at home anymore. She was living out her dream. Except, her dream hadn't included meeting a police officer. It hadn't included sleeping in a stranger's house. It hadn't included not having a permanent place of her own.

Hopefully, today would be a *gut* day. Hopefully, today would be the day she found a place to rent. Hopefully, today would be the day she would find a job.

One could always hope.

She glanced down at her clothing before answering the knock. She'd slept in the same clothes she'd worn last night. Now, she wished she'd had the forethought to bring a nightgown. But only so much had fit inside her backpack. Even if she had thought of it, there was a *gut* chance she may not have brought it along.

"Good morning." It was the officer. Instead of his uniform, he was dressed in casual shorts and a T-shirt. He looked like any other guy on the street. She liked him this way better. It felt less threatening somehow.

"Good morning."

"My mom said to let you know breakfast is almost ready."

Susan frowned. "What time is it?"

"Eight."

"Eight o'clock?" Her jaw sagged.

He smiled with a nod.

"*Ach*, it's so late."

"You're probably used to going to bed earlier than you did last night. And then the added stress of not knowing where you were going to stay..." He shrugged. "Don't worry about it. It's all good."

"I should have helped with breakfast."

He laughed. "You're a guest in this house. My mom wouldn't have let you help with breakfast if you begged her." He gestured to the bathroom across the hallway. "Feel free to freshen up if you need to."

Susan nodded and thanked him.

When he continued down the hallway and into the kitchen, Susan did her best not to notice how nicely his black T-shirt hugged his shoulders and upper arms. Which inadvertently reminded her how wonderful it had felt to be held in Joshua's arms. *Stop it. He's. A. Cheater.* She did her best to refocus her thoughts.

Thankfully, she'd had the forethought to snatch her toothbrush. She hurried to, as the officer had put it, "freshen up" before breakfast. She was almost afraid to look in the mirror. Who knew what she looked like after a night of sleeping in a foreign bed? She breathed a sigh of relief. *Not too bad.*

She needed to change into a fresh outfit before facing the world again. Since she'd be looking for a job and a place to stay today, she opted for the stretchy skirt she'd found at the thrift store. She'd been amazed at how nice it fit when she'd tried it on. It was so light, it almost felt like she was wearing nothing. Why would anyone want to get rid of such a lovely article of clothing?

Once dressed, she made her way to the kitchen, where the officer, his mom, and a man who Susan assumed to be his dad sat at the table chatting.

The officer stood from the table when she entered the room. "Would you like a cup of coffee?"

"Yes. Thank you."

Susan had met the officer's *mamm* briefly last night, but they hadn't chatted much due to the late hour. From the few moments they had spoken, though, Susan could tell the woman was kind. She gestured for Susan to sit down across from the officer.

"We never actually got a chance to properly meet each other last night." The officer slid a cup of coffee in her direction, along with cute matching ceramic containers holding sugar and cream. "My name is Blaze. And these are my parents, Joe and Mindy."

Blaze? Ach, she'd never heard that as a name before. She nodded. "Nice to meet you. I'm Sue."

"Sue. So, Suzette? Susan? Suzanne?" Blaze was fishing for her full name, no doubt. Must be the police officer inside him.

"You can call me Sue."

"Blaze, don't interrogate the woman, for Pete's sake," his father said.

Mindy set a plate of scrambled eggs on the table, along with a frying pan of bacon. "Blaze tells us that you're Amish."

"Was Amish," Blaze corrected.

Susan nodded. "Yes."

"I've read a few of those Amish novels. Are they anything like real life for you?" Mindy asked.

"I wouldn't know. I've never read one. My sisters are the readers in the family."

"That's interesting, dear. Well, I can explain," his mother continued.

Blaze shot her an apologetic smile.

"They talk about the shunning and all that, when a person leaves the Amish. Is that how it is? And do the young people really get together and sing in the barns and all that?"

Susan smiled. It probably sounded like a funny thing to *Englischers*. She wasn't sure what *all that* referred to, but the rest seemed pretty accurate. "That sounds about right."

"Mindy, why don't you let her eat now?" Joe urged.

Blaze motioned for Susan to take food. She helped herself to a little of everything.

"Will you be shunned now?" Mindy asked.

"Mom." Blaze laid his hand on his mother's arm and shook his head. "That's a personal question."

Susan raised a thankful smile in his direction.

"Let's just eat, Mindy," Joe said.

Susan was already a couple of bites into her meal

before she realized they hadn't prayed yet. She'd almost said something but refrained. Perhaps that was a normal thing for the *Englisch*? She whispered her own prayer of thankfulness under her breath. She couldn't help but give thanks for meeting Blaze and his family. They'd given her a roof over her head, a place to sleep, and a plateful of food. She needed to acknowledge those blessings.

She surmised there wouldn't be a closing prayer either, when Blaze's father had finished his meal and declared he was headed out the door for the day.

She tried to help clear the table and wash dishes, but Mindy would have none of it.

"Blaze says you have a lot to do today, so I won't keep you from it. You are welcome to join us for a meal any time, dear."

Susan smiled her gratefulness. "I appreciate the invitation."

"You ready to head out?" Her attention swung to Blaze, who held up keys.

"But you're not coming. You need to rest still." She'd already retrieved her bag from his room.

"Trust me, I won't be able to sleep until I know you're settled," Blaze asserted.

"He isn't kidding," Mindy commented. "That boy's always been a protector."

Susan immediately thought of her brothers. Nathaniel, especially, had always been overprotective. No doubt he was freaking out about now.

"Let's go." Blaze motioned to the door. "The sooner we get you settled, the sooner I can take my nap."

"Really. You don't have to come with me."

"I insist. You won't talk me out of it." He led the way to a fancy sports car.

"I thought we were walking."

"You don't want to ride in my Camaro?" He looked genuinely offended, and she almost laughed.

"I've never been in such a fancy car."

"Well, in that case, maybe we'll go for a little spin first."

She hesitated. At this rate, she'd never find a place to stay. "Maybe I should just walk by myself."

He clenched his shirt near his heart. "You really know how to hurt a man's pride."

"It is not *gut* to be proud."

He chuckled. "I promise it won't take long. Besides, I have a surprise for you."

She frowned. "A surprise?"

"It's a good one. I promise. Just trust me."

Trust me. Ach, she'd heard that before. From Joshua. She'd trusted him alright. Only to be let down hard and fast.

Blaze opened the door and she slid in, setting her backpack between her feet. The car smelled *wunderbaar*.

He slipped into the leather seat on the other side. "Seat belt."

She clicked the safety belt into place.

He maneuvered the car out of the driveway and down the street.

"How did you get your name?" she asked.

"My parents." His teasing smile grew.

She took the baseball cap he had sitting between them and swatted his arm with it. "You know what I mean."

He chuckled, took the hat from her, and put it on her head. "Hey, you look cute with a hat on."

Her face suddenly felt warm. "Your name," she reminded, adjusting the hat until it felt comfortable.

"My dad is a firefighter." Blaze smiled. "My sister's name is Ember."

"Kind of like Amber."

"Yes, but with an E. Pull down the visor and look in the mirror."

She did as he suggested.

"Have you ever worn a baseball cap?"

She shook her head. "No."

"What do you think?"

She shrugged. "I don't know."

"It looks good on you. Keep it." He winked in her direction.

"Oh, I couldn't."

"Sure, you can. I have plenty of other hats, so I won't miss it." He turned onto one of the roads that went out into the country. "Hang on." A wicked grin crossed his face as the car began to pick up speed faster and faster.

Ach, everything out the window turned into a blur. She gripped the door and the arm rest, as the back of her chest pressed flush with the seat.

Blaze passed every other vehicle, including a police car. He chuckled. "That was my coworker."

"You don't get in trouble for driving too fast?" She glanced into the side mirror.

Lights flashed and a siren sounded behind them, startling her.

Blaze laughed. "Nah."

"Are you going to pull over?"

"Yeah, I'll drive onto the shoulder up ahead." He did as he said, then rolled the window down as the uniformed officer approached on her side.

"Going a little fast there, weren't you, Jackson?" The officer wore an amused look, and his gaze bounced back and forth from Susan to Blaze. "I see.

Showing off for the lady, huh?"

"What good does it do to have a fast car, if you can't drive fast?"

"Right?" The other officer chuckled, then winked. "But you really need to slow down. I clocked you at 92."

Blaze whistled. "Ah, not too bad."

"If you're on the Kentucky Speedway. Really, Blaze. I'd hate to see you get in trouble. I'll let you off with a warning, this time." The officer shook his head. "Well, you two enjoy your day. And stay safe."

By the officer's look, Susan guessed he'd thought they were a courting couple. Blaze hadn't set him straight otherwise.

"We will." Before the other officer reached his vehicle, Blaze had put the car in gear and made a U-turn. The tires squealed and spewed rocks. "Oh, yeah."

"You like driving fast, don't you?"

"Oh, man. It's such a rush."

"I've never driven a car," she admitted.

He stared at her. "Never?"

She shook her head.

"Really?" Unbelief flashed across his face.

She nodded.

"Do you plan on learning? Getting your license and all that?"

"I don't...I'm not sure. I just thought that I would walk everywhere."

"Not a good plan for Indiana. You're liable to get poured on."

"I can buy an umbrella." She shrugged. "I really don't have any way to practice driving."

"You don't have any non-Amish relatives?"

"No."

"How about friends?"

"Not really. They are neighbors and drivers for our family. I couldn't ask them, even if I wanted to."

"Because word would get back to your family?"

She nodded.

"Well, if you want, I can teach you."

Her eyes flew wide. "Oh, I couldn't ask you to do that."

"You're not asking. I'm volunteering. Seriously."

Emotion clogged her throat. "You would do that for me?"

"We'd probably use my mom's car to practice in. After you get the hang of it and get your driver's license, you could take this thing for a spin."

Excitement bubbled in her chest as she thought of the *Englisch* girls driving past the farm. What would it be like if she and Blaze drove past her folks' farm with her in the driver's seat? They wouldn't even recognize her. Especially if she was wearing her *Englisch* clothes and Blaze's baseball cap. "Really? You would let me drive this?"

"I've always been game for an adventure." He winked. "Part of the reason why I became a cop."

She sucked in a long breath, then released it. "Okay, then."

"Okay? You want to learn to drive?"

"I'm warning you right now that I know absolutely nothing."

He guffawed. "I believe it. But I'm sure you know way more about handling a horse than I ever will."

"*Jah*, probably." She glanced up at the road and noticed they were heading back into town. "Where are we going?"

"Remember that surprise I mentioned earlier?" He pulled into the motel's parking lot.

She frowned. "Why are we here?"

"This is it. This is your surprise. I talked the manager into renting you a room." He raised his eyebrows twice. "It helps that he's a friend of the family." He parked the car.

"You got me a room? To rent?" Her excitement was barely restrained.

At his nod, she squealed. Then she leaned over the console and hugged this wonderful man. "Thank you, Blaze!"

FOURTEEN

Joshua finally found the desire to open Lissa's letter. The truth was, he'd been upset with her because she'd ruined his chances with Susan. Which was the most ridiculous thing that had ever come to his mind. Lissa had nothing to do with Susan's abandonment. *Nee*, the fault rested squarely on his own shoulders. But his secret would have remained hidden, had Lissa's letter not arrived. So somehow, his mind wanted to shift the blame. But he knew better.

The sooner he cut ties with his former *aldi*, the sooner he could continue with his life here in Indiana. *Ach*, how had he come to these thoughts? He sounded so callous and uncaring, even to himself. It was almost as if the moment he'd decided that he and Lissa weren't right for each other, his mind flipped a one-eighty.

He had to keep a steady head and remember that

he wasn't the only one with thoughts and feelings in this equation. He'd always felt he needed to protect Lissa from negative emotions. Now, he would be the one projecting those negative emotions onto her.

I've become a jerk, Lord. Help me not to be. Give me the right words so I don't hurt anybody. Of course, he'd already hurt Susan. The thought pained his heart.

He let the letter fall open between his hands, and his eyes moved over the words. He found himself scanning most of it, the part about her *schweschder* and the baby and diaper changes. Until something of interest caught his eye.

How long are you and your folks planning to be in Indiana?

Ach, she thought they were just visiting? If that was the case, she hadn't read his letter yet, which he'd already figured. Perhaps he should just rewrite the letter and send it to her today. She'd likely get it quicker than when she arrived home, which was still at least a week away, by the sound of it. Then he could just tell her to disregard the letter he'd left with his folks.

He rummaged through the small desk in the dawdi haus and located some lined paper, then found a pen.

Hi, Lissa.

I'm not sure who told you about my family coming to Indiana, but we're not here for just a visit. We're moving here permanently.

With that being the case, I think it's best that we end our courtship. Long-distance relationships seldom work out. Feel free to let other men court you. I won't be holding you back.

He paused. Should he tell her about Susan? *Nee.* She didn't need to know that he'd already moved on. That knowledge might just cause her unnecessary grief, and getting this news would be difficult enough for her.

I hope you have a nice life there in Pennsylvania and find someone worthy of you to share your life with.

Your Friend,

Joshua Beachy

He folded the letter and stuck it in an envelope, then sighed in relief once he'd stamped it and sent it on its way. He would have preferred to call Lissa, but she hadn't included a phone number. A letter would have to do.

Now, he could properly pursue Susan and let her know that he'd officially ended things.

~

Susan sat on the bed in her tiny studio apartment, smiling in contentment. The space was small but contained everything she needed. A refrigerator, a stove, a coffee maker, a microwave, and even a television, which she could do without.

She could turn cartwheels, she was so happy. But doing cartwheels in this little space would probably end in her breaking something. So, she opted for wiggling her legs and pumping her fists in the air instead. She'd already danced around the tiny, carpeted area.

She planned to walk through town today to find out if any of the shops were hiring. Blaze said he'd stop by later during his break to say hello and see how she was doing. It was kind of nice having a cop for a friend.

He'd said they would begin her driving lessons after she'd secured a job and figured out her work schedule. One thing she realized she would need to do was buy more clothes. Living Amish was simple as far as clothing went. She wore a cape dress every day. Blue. Green. Purple. Grey. But it was always a dress. One essential item. Now, she had to decide to wear either jeans or a skirt and pick out a different top to go with it each day. And since she only owned three shirts, her choices couldn't vary much.

Were there even any clothing stores in Versailles? She thought she'd remembered seeing clothes at the dollar stores before. She could stop in at the closest one, which was easily within walking distance. But she'd wait until she secured a job before she could spend money on clothes.

~

If Joshua stayed in this home another minute, he was going to go crazy. After the family had learned of Susan's departure, the atmosphere had changed. Friendly welcoming smiles had been replaced with frowns and furrowed brows. It was downright depressing. He couldn't blame them, though.

When his brother Josiah had been reported missing and likely dead, it had turned his family upside down. Since he'd been the youngest, he didn't remember all the suffering his parents had gone through, but he understood it in part. He recalled standing outside *Mamm* and *Daed's* bedroom door and the two of them crying and consoling one another. Learning their child could be deceased was the most difficult thing his folks had faced. And not knowing for sure and for certain was even worse, in a way, than actually knowing.

He couldn't help but wonder if similar thoughts were going through the Miller parents' minds. When a baptized member left the *g'may*, they were to be put in the *Bann* if they didn't return with a repentant heart. If that happened, Joshua wouldn't be able to socialize with Susan when he found her in the *Englisch* world. He was to admonish her to return to the fold, or else face the consequences of an eternity in hell. He would be forced to cut all ties with her and leave her in the devil's hands. That was what his Pennsylvania church district had believed.

He didn't like that thought one bit. But maybe the rules were different here. Likely not, by the family's reaction.

Susan's folks had called every family member they could think of, hoping she'd just gone to stay with one of them. But her letter had clearly indicated she had planned to become *Englisch*. They'd contacted every driver to see if one of them had taken Susan somewhere and learned she'd been dropped off in Versailles. They'd hired a driver to take them into the nearby town but had come up with nothing thus far.

Declining to go to work with *Daed*, Nathaniel, and his father had been a mistake. He had planned to go looking for Susan on his own. How could he do that, though, without divulging his whereabouts? If his and Susan's mothers thought he was going to look for her, they'd likely want to come along. Notwithstanding, they'd have a hundred questions he wouldn't be able to answer.

But maybe he could go to visit his brother first. He could stay there for just a little while, then have the driver take him into town. That way, no one would be suspicious. He hoped.

~

"*Bruder*!" Josiah engulfed Joshua in a bear hug the moment he stepped out of the vehicle. "Perfect timing. I'm going to see Sammy."

"Sammy?"

"Sammy Eicher. Remember my friend Michael?"

Joshua shook his head.

"I guess you were too young to remember back then." Josiah shrugged. "Sammy is Michael's *grossdawdi*."

"I see."

"A bunch of us guys get together about once a week and hang out. You should come." Josiah frowned. "Aren't you staying with the Millers? I would have thought Nathaniel would have invited you."

Joshua grunted.

His brother's eyebrow arched. "What was *that* all about?"

"I'm not exactly Nathaniel's favorite person."

Josiah chuckled. "He didn't care for Jaden at first, either. He'll eventually warm up to you."

Joshua blew out a breath. "I doubt it."

"What did you do to get on his bad side?"

"Where should I start?"

"That bad, huh?"

"I admit that I may have been a tad bit spiteful."

"Spiteful?" His brother's eyes widened.

"Maybe not the best choice of word. But he warned me to stay away from his sister. I did the opposite. On purpose."

Josiah laughed out loud. "You're definitely a Beachy."

"Apparently. I'm trying *not to* uphold that reputation."

"Good luck, *bruder*. Good luck." He chuckled.

"Thanks."

Josiah squeezed his shoulder. "Come on. Let's go say hello to Nora and the *kinner* before we head over to Sammy's."

"How many do you have now?"

"Five altogether." Josiah's grin stretched across his face.

Joshua had never seen his brother with this must enthusiasm for life. Someday, he hoped he'd be as happy as his brother. Settled down. Married to...*Susan*?

A half hour later, Joshua found himself sitting

alone at Sammy Eicher's dining table, enjoying a slice of Kayla Miller's famous potpie. Michael and Josiah had hauled all the *kinner* outside to release energy, they'd said.

"The best, *ain't not*?" Sammy's eyes sparkled as he walked into the room.

"*Jah*, it's *gut*." The potpie really was delicious, but he couldn't muster the same enthusiasm as Sammy. Not when Susan was somewhere unknown to him. He couldn't help but worry about her. What if she got caught up with the wrong crowd?

"Wanna talk about what's on your mind?"

Joshua sighed. "I'd better not."

"If I had to wager a guess, I'd say problems involving a *maedel*." Sammy took a seat at the table.

Joshua chuckled. "Good guess."

"We've all had our share of those." Sammy reached a hand over and touched his arm briefly. "Whatever it is, give it to *Der Herr, sohn*. Let Him handle it for you. He cares about the things you care about."

"So, you think I should do nothing?"

Sammy shrugged. "I can't say what you should do other than to pray. Ask God to show you what He would have you do."

Joshua nodded.

"Do you mind if I pray with you?" Sammy smiled.

"You mean, right now?" He set his fork on the empty plate.

Sammy nodded.

"Okay."

When Sammy bowed his head, Joshua followed suit. "Oh, wise and gracious Father above. Thank You for Your goodness and Your great love toward us. You know the cry of our hearts. You know what we need before we even ask for it. I come before You today to ask for guidance and wisdom for my new friend, Joshua Beachy. Show him Your will and the path You want him to walk in, Lord. Then give him the courage and strength to do what is right. We ask these things in the wonderful name of Your precious Son, Jesus. And we thank You for hearing our prayer. Amen."

Joshua finished with his own quiet Amen. "Thank you. I'm beginning to think the good things my *bruder* has said about you are true."

Sammy swatted the air in front of him. "Don't believe any of it. I am nothing. I only share what *Der Herr* has already given me. Save your praise for Him, *bu*."

Jah. Josiah had been right. Sammy was truly an inspiration.

FIFTEEN

Pen poised in hand, Susan's brow furrowed as she hovered over the small stack of job applications she'd accumulated today. How was she going to fill these out? She'd gone through and written her name and the hotel's address on each of them. But now, the application asked for other information she didn't have.

Phone number? She had a phone in the room, but to her knowledge it was only to make calls, not to receive them. She supposed she could ask the hotel manager if she could use theirs. But that might be awkward.

Email address? She didn't have one.

Social security number? She had none.

Name of high school attended? None.

College? None.

Job history and skills? Well, she'd worked at home

her entire life. She had filled in at Silas and Kayla's store a couple of times and she manned Emily's roadside stand, but she didn't think that qualified. Did it?

How much money do you expect to make? How was she supposed to answer that? Enough to get by and be able to purchase what she needed? How much was that even?

An hour later, she glanced through each job application, grimacing at all of the blank parts. Who in their right mind was going to hire someone as uneducated and inexperienced as her? Especially since she didn't know the first thing about computers.

A knock on the door drew her attention and she peeked out the window. She opened the door.

"Blaze." It was nice to see a familiar face. She hoped the neighbors didn't think she was in trouble. It wasn't every day a uniformed policeman stood outside one's door.

"I'm on my lunch break."

"Lunch? At five o'clock?"

He confirmed with a nod. "Just wanted to stop in and see how things are going."

She pointed to the table. "Trying to fill out job applications." She shook her head. "Nobody's going to hire me."

"Why not?" He frowned.

"Well, for one thing, I don't even have a phone number where they can reach me at."

"That's easy, just buy one. Do you have any extra money you can spare?"

She grimaced. "Some. How much?"

"Probably won't be more than fifty dollars for a simple flip phone and a month of service."

"But don't I need a credit card?"

"Nope. You just pay as you go. When you run out of service, just go buy a twenty-dollar refill card. Twenty bucks a month should be easy to swing once you have a job."

Hope filled her. "Okay. I think I can spare fifty dollars if it helps me get a job." She smiled now. "Where can I get one of those flip phones?"

"One of the dollar stores should have them. Maybe even IGA." He thumbed over his shoulder. "I can take you there now, if you want to go. Have you eaten dinner yet?"

"*Ach*, no. I haven't made a trip to the store yet."

Blaze frowned. "You *have* eaten *something* today, right?"

"I had breakfast at your house, remember?"

"That was many hours ago." He shook his head. "You've gotta eat. Come on, let's go grab some food and we'll pick up your phone while we're out."

"Don't you have to be back to work?"

He glanced at his wristwatch. "I have some time, but we'll have to get fast food. Or, if you want pizza, we can put in an order and have them make it while we drive to get your phone."

Excitement sparked. "Pizza?"

"Pizza, it is." He chuckled. "Come on. My treat."

~

Joshua stared out the car window, anxious to get to town. He'd ended up staying at Sammy's, then at Josiah's, later than he'd expected. Fortunately, the evening air was pleasant and there were several hours of daylight still left.

He really didn't have a set plan, except that he'd arranged a time and place to be picked up by his driver. Hopefully, his search would prove fruitful, but he kept his expectations low. The chances that Susan would be outside, that he would see her, and that he'd be able to recognize her without her Amish clothing, or with *Englisch* clothing, rather, were slim. But what else could he do?

He didn't have much to go on, except that Susan had to be staying somewhere and that she would be seeking out a job so she could provide for herself.

Since Versailles was the closest town, it made the most sense. And he was pretty confident this was where she was because her folks had called all their drivers. The one who had driven Susan yesterday had dropped her off here in town. So that was something, at least.

He planned to begin his search by having the driver drop him off where Susan had been let off yesterday. From there, he had no idea but to pray and use his instincts. *Please guide me to her,* Gott.

But what if he actually found her? Then what? What was he going to say to her? He knew the typical "Come back to the People or you're going to hell" plea would not work on her. Besides, he was pretty sure that leaving the Amish didn't result in a future doomed to eternal fire and damnation. If that were true, surely God would have made a lot more folks be born Amish, right? It made sense in his mind, anyway.

Nee, he wouldn't mention coming home at all. If he didn't mention it, maybe he could keep an open door to their relationship. But then again, last time he saw her, she wanted nothing to do with him. Either way, he had to set her straight on the subject of Lissa. She deserved to at least know the truth of the matter.

His heart had already been free when he'd kissed Susan.

If she didn't accept that truth, then there was really

nothing else he could do. He wasn't going to force her to be with him. She had to want it. Like she'd wanted his kiss. And he knew she'd wanted it just as much as he had.

If only she wanted him.

SIXTEEN

Susan couldn't contain her smile as she stared down at the phone in her hand. She actually owned a cell phone. Granted, it was the old flip kind, but it was still a novelty to her. Now, she could fill out the phone number part on her applications. She probably wouldn't have to worry about any unsolicited calls because they would either be from perspective employers, her landlords, who she planned to give her number to just in case they needed to get ahold of her, or Blaze.

"Do you think you can figure out how to set that thing up?" Blaze smiled before taking another bite of his pepperoni pizza.

"You said it should be easy, right? And the instructions are inside the box."

"Right. If you can't figure it out, call me from your room phone and I'll come over when I get a chance."

"You don't do this sort of thing for every person you find walking down the street, do you?"

He chuckled. "Definitely not. And you're not just anyone."

"But I'm nobody special." She shrugged.

"Wash your mouth out with soap, girl!"

"What?" She laughed.

"You heard me. Don't ever say you're nobody special." He shook his head. "And I was kidding about the washing your mouth out part. Sort of. But don't do that. Soap tastes nasty."

"You sound like you know by experience."

"Oh, I had my mouth washed out a few times when I was a boy." Mischief sparkled in his eyes.

"Why?"

"Saying bad words. My mother did not like that. Needless to say, I still watch my language when I'm around her."

"I see." She studied him. "You kind of remind me of my brother Paul."

"Ah, so you have a brother?"

"Three, actually."

"Older or younger?"

"Two older, one younger."

"There's four of you, then?"

"No, only one of me," she teased. "There are

actually six of us children."

"So, three boys and three girls." He nodded. "Are you the youngest girl?"

"No, I'm in the middle."

"That explains it." He chuckled.

"Explains what?" Her brow lowered.

"Why you're out and about exploring the outside world. The oldest and the youngest seem to get the most attention. The oldest just because they're first and the youngest because they're the baby. They both get spoiled, but the oldest usually has more weight on their shoulders. So, the middle child sometimes ends up feeling left out or even forgotten. Your brother Paul, is he a middle child too?"

"How did you know?"

"Well, middle children sometimes do drastic things to get attention. They're more likely to be the rebels."

"Wow. I guess I never really thought of it that way, but you're right. I always looked up to my oldest brother, Silas. He always seemed so good and wise. And my oldest sister, Martha, was always bossy."

"And does the youngest seem to get preferential treatment?"

She thought of Emily. "Well, I think she got away with more stuff. Like when she brought the kittens into the house. Mom and Dad never would have allowed it before. But she acted like her heart would break if they had to stay outside." Susan rolled her eyes.

Blaze laughed. "Yeah, that's how it goes." He glanced at his watch, then stood up. "Speaking of going. I've gotta run. Thanks for joining me for lunch. Take the leftovers home with you."

"Okay. Thank you for helping me get my phone and all that. And thanks for the pizza."

"No problem. I wrote my number down for you, so call or text me when you get your new number, okay?"

"Okay." She smiled as he quickly paid, then rushed out the door to his car. She had already known he wasn't going to have time to drop her off at the motel. The pizza place was just down the road, within easy walking distance, so she didn't mind at all.

She waved as he drove off. She really enjoyed spending time with Blaze. He was a nice guy, for sure. But something was missing.

~

Joshua did a doubletake as his driver drove past the new pizza parlor. Not because he'd noticed the uniformed police officer, which he did, but because of the woman with the officer. She bore an uncanny resemblance to Susan.

But surely Susan wouldn't be accompanying a police officer to supper. And she certainly would not have been laughing and carrying on with him the way this woman was. Would she?

He'd never seen Susan in *Englisch* clothes, nor had he seen her with her hair down during the day, so he couldn't determine anything by that. The woman's smile seemed identical to Susan's, though.

He shook his head in an attempt to clear his thoughts. The mind was a powerful thing. It was like he wanted to see Susan so badly that he was imagining her being somewhere she wasn't. Surely, upon further inspection—if he'd had the time and his driver had stopped—he would have confirmed that his thoughts were indeed *ferhoodled*.

Nah, the notion of Susan dining with a policeman was as ludicrous as his old scaredy-cat buggy horse wading through a creek. *Jah*, it was *possible*, but the probability of it actually happening was likely one out of a hundred. Or a thousand even.

~

It had been three hours. Three hours. Joshua had walked through most of the town. No sign of Susan whatsoever. But he wasn't about to give up. He'd continue his search tomorrow. And then the next day.

However long it took to find Susan.

He may have to return home for the night, but he wasn't about to give up searching. *Nee*, he wouldn't stop looking until he found her.

God, please just keep her safe.

SEVENTEEN

"Any luck with the job search?" Blaze's mother asked from across the table.

It had been a week since Susan turned in her applications and she'd only heard back from a couple of places. Neither sounded too promising. What was she going to do if she couldn't get a job?

"No, nothing yet." She sighed. "Thank you for having me over for dinner again. It's nice to have company."

"Blaze insisted. He knows you're new to town." Mindy smiled. "And since Joe is out with the guys tonight, you're keeping me company too."

"Does your daughter live around here?"

"Ember lives in the greater Cincinnati area. She comes to visit some weekends, but she's pretty busy. I don't know how much Blaze has told you about her, but she has a small family. Joe and I are always happy when she brings the grandchildren over."

Susan thought about her folks and how they always lit up when her nieces and nephews came to visit. How was everybody doing back home?

"Someday I'm hoping Blaze can find that kind of happiness," Mindy remarked.

Susan thought about her friend. "Blaze is a kind man."

"He likes you, you know."

"*Jah*, I like him too."

"I mean as *more* than a friend."

Susan's breath stole away. "No. We're just friends."

"Maybe for now, but I think there's potential for something more. He admires you."

Ach. Susan hoped Blaze's mother was wrong. She wasn't looking for a romantic relationship. They were just too complicated. She enjoyed the friendship she had with Blaze, and something more would mess it up. Besides, he was *Englisch*.

"Speaking of Blaze, I think he just pulled up." Mindy smiled, then looked at the clock on the wall. "Yep. His shift just ended a little while ago."

"Hey." Blaze walked through the doorway with his usual handsome grin, and his gaze connected with Susan's. "Whenever you're ready, I'll give you a ride home. I'm gonna go grab a shower real quick."

"How was your shift, son?"

"Okay. But I'm tired."

Susan spoke up. "We can go now, if you'd like."

"After my shower." He winked in her direction. "I've got something I want to talk to you about."

He continued down the hall to his bedroom, then she heard the bathroom door click shut and the shower turn on.

All of a sudden, she felt nervous. What did Blaze want to talk to her about? Was he going to ask her to go on a date? And if he did, what would she say? She almost felt obligated to say yes. He'd already done so much for her.

If she declined, though, it would seem like she was ungrateful. But she wasn't ungrateful at all. Without Blaze's help, she probably wouldn't have found a place to rent. She wouldn't have a phone that possible employers could call. She wouldn't have an occasional meal companion.

Without Blaze, she likely would have given up and gone back home.

Not ten minutes later, Blaze emerged fresh-shaven and smelling wonderful *gut*. His dark hair was *ferhoodled*, but it looked good on him.

What was wrong with her? Any woman would feel honored to have a date with him. He was kind, handsome, hardworking. Basically, the whole package.

He jingled his keys. "You ready?" His voice held an undetectable timbre to it. Like he was referring to more than being ready to go home.

She couldn't speak, so she nodded.

The drive back to her place was quiet. Blaze was obviously exhausted. She was lost in thought.

He pulled into the small parking lot and cut the engine. "May I come inside for a sec?"

He'd never asked to enter her apartment, so his request came as a bit of a surprise. But she trusted Blaze. "*Jah*, sure. Would you like some coffee?"

"I'd love some if you have decaf."

"I do." She led the way inside. "You can have a seat." She gestured to her lone chair.

He sat down and yawned.

"You look tired." She lifted a small smile and filled a coffee filter with fresh grounds.

"Yeah, I am."

A few moments later, she slid a full mug in his direction.

"Thanks." He took a sip. "You know, I already had coffee earlier today. I stopped in at the little café downtown."

"It's a cute place."

"Do you like it?"

"Well, I've never had coffee there because I'm trying to be frugal with my dollars." She sighed. "If I could just find someone who would give me a chance." She wouldn't let her emotions overwhelm her. She would not.

"That's kind of what I wanted to talk to you about."

Hope sparked to life. "Did you hear about a place that's hiring?"

"I talked to the owners of the coffee shop. You have a job there starting tomorrow if you want it."

Tears rushed to the surface. "You got me a job?"

He shrugged. "It's a foot in the door. You'll have to do the work."

"*Ach*, Blaze! You are the best kind of friend. Thank you."

He reached for her hand and held it gently. "I'd like to be more." His eyes searched hers.

Her cheeks warmed under his examination. She felt like snatching her hand away, but she couldn't. Not after all he'd done for her. She shook her head. "Blaze..."

"There's someone else, isn't there? An Amish guy?" He lifted a small smile.

"It's...complicated." She shrugged.

"Is that why you left?"

"No. And yes. That's why I left when I did."

He sighed. "Why is it the good ones are always taken?"

She stared at him. "You're a good one and you're not taken."

He chuckled. "Thanks for saying that. I'm not sure everyone would agree."

"We all have our issues."

"Some more than others, though."

"I find no fault in you."

"Wow, you really are one of a kind." He smiled, but she sensed pain behind it. "Susan, I'm divorced, and I have a kid I hardly ever see."

"*Ach*. I never would have guessed. You're so young."

"Not that young. Old enough to have already made a mess of my life."

Her heart ached for him. "I'm sorry."

"Not as sorry as I am, trust me." He drained his coffee, then stood from the table. "I'd better go."

"Blaze?"

He turned at her voice.

"If it means anything to you, I still think you're a good guy."

He nodded and hung his head. "Thanks." Then he walked out the door.

After the lights of his vehicle faded, Susan broke down and cried for the brokenness she saw in his entire being.

Gott, please heal Blaze's heart and show him Your unconditional love.

~

As Joshua leaned down to don his work boots, he admitted that the search for Susan had been disheartening so far. But he believed that *Der Herr* would lead him to her in His perfect timing. It would be nice, though, if *Gott* would let him know when that would be. That way, he wouldn't be wasting so much time and money. Of course, if he found her, it would all be worth it.

But weren't there instances where people lived in the same town for decades and never saw each other? They just never crossed paths at the same time. The thought was crazy. Yet, he *had to* find her. Surely *Der Herr* would not make him wait decades to find her. Would He?

"You know where she is, don't you?" Nathaniel entered the mudroom.

If only. "No, I don't." He continued lacing up his boots.

"Then where have you been running off to every

day? Or is there an *aldi* number three somewhere?"

Joshua growled, then forced his lips together. *Do not respond. Just walk away. Just walk away.* He forced himself to rein in his emotions as he stood and took steps away from the object of his ire.

Nathaniel caught up to him and waved an envelope in front of his face. "Don't you want your *schatzi's* letter?"

Joshua snatched his mail from Nathaniel's hand and continued onward. He needed to go for a nice long walk—as far away from Nathaniel Miller as possible. Oh, for the day when *Daed* would find a place of their own! While he was grateful for *most* of the Miller family and their hospitality, Nathaniel was an entirely different ball of wax. Joshua didn't know what he'd done—other than exist—that had landed him on Nathaniel's list of "Most Hated People." Of course, he hadn't helped by directly defying Susan's brother's orders. But still.

He continued his trek and finally stopped near the place where he and Susan had kissed. *Ach, Susan. Why did you have to leave?* The sound of the trickling water from the creek somehow brought a calm to his anxious soul. It was almost like a whisper from *Gott* saying all would be well with Susan. *Denki* for keeping her, Lord.

Once he was certain he was alone, he tore open Lissa's letter. Truth was, he was both dreading it and looking forward to it. This would be the conclusion of their relationship and he could now, in good conscience, fully pursue Susan.

He planted himself on a rock and allowed his gaze to settle on the page.

Dear Joshua,

Needless to say, your letter came as a shock to me. You never said your family might be moving, and I'm sad that you never mentioned it to me.

About what you said regarding long-distance relationships. I think they can work out. And honestly, I can't see myself dating anyone else but you. It matters not to me whether you want to get married and live here in Pennsylvania or in Indiana. By what I've heard from your folks, Indiana is very pretty and the community is friendly. It doesn't sound like living there would be a hardship. We can do that if that's what you'd like. We can always come back to visit my family in Pennsylvania.

I already spoke to Mom and Dad and they're fine with the idea of me moving on and creating a life with you in Indiana. Dad said he could find a replacement for me at the furniture store. The more I think about it, the more excited I'm becoming.

I think a wedding this fall would be best.

Looking forward to seeing you again.

Yours alone,

Lissa

"*What*?" Joshua hadn't meant to shout the word. "No, no, no, no, no."

He splayed his hand over his face and groaned loudly. What a disaster. *Ach*, he should have told Lissa about Susan. Now, what was he going to do?

God? Direction, please.

He needed to talk to Sammy. Now.

EIGHTEEN

S usan enjoyed her new job immensely. She got along well with her coworkers and had learned the ropes fairly quickly. Blaze stopped by daily for coffee—something she suspected he already did before she began working there. Which made her wonder. Had he specifically chosen this place so they would cross paths often? The possibility warmed her heart. He had been a *gut* friend to her. She wanted to return the favor somehow.

She thought on his revelation last week. Her heart couldn't help but ache for him. She had so many questions. What had transpired in his life up till now? Where were his wife and child? Did they live around here? Was there any hope of them working things out and getting back together? Surely, his child needed a father.

She planned to sit down with Blaze and have a

heart-to-heart with him. If nothing else, to at least find out what had happened to land him in this place. Perhaps *Gott* could salvage his family. She would pray for that.

~

Lissa's letter had wrecked Joshua's plans for the day. He'd wanted to go searching for Susan again, but how could he do that now? When Lissa thought they were still a happy, thriving couple and was, by the sound of it, making plans to move to Indiana and marry him.

Apparently, subtlety was *not* his field of expertise. By far.

What he needed was wisdom. And he knew exactly where to go for it. Sammy Eicher.

"What did you say to her in your letter?" Sammy picked up a curry comb and began combing his old gelding, Dr. Seuss.

"I said that I think it's best that we ended our courtship. Something about long-distance relationships not working out. I told her to let other men court her and that I wasn't going to be holding her back. And I said that I hope she has a nice life in Pennsylvania and that she finds someone worthy of her to share her life with. Something to that effect." Joshua shrugged. It had sounded *gut* to him.

"You're right. You're not good with subtlety."

"Thanks. But what do I do?"

"It looks like you're going to have to spill the truth. Tell her how you honestly feel. And that you've found another *maedel*."

Joshua's eyes widened. "How in the world did you know that?"

Sammy shrugged. "I have my ways."

Probably one of his brothers or Nathaniel had mentioned it to him.

"What should I say?"

"Don't know. But I'm willing to be your sounding board."

Joshua chuckled. "I get the feeling you're everybody's sounding board."

"I have yet to be a sounding board for the leaders of the community."

Joshua smiled. "They're probably afraid to ask."

Sammy laughed out loud now. "You may be right about that."

"Okay, how about this? Um...Dear Lissa—"

"Cut the 'dear.' It sounds too affectionate. You're trying to break up with her, so every word needs to count."

"Okay, no 'dear'..." He took a deep breath and continued. "Lissa, A relationship between us isn't going to work—"

"Aaahnn." Sammy sounded like one of those game buzzers. "That's too subtle. You aren't *gut* with subtlety, remember?"

"Dear Lissa—*ach*—no dear. Lissa, I'm breaking up with you?"

"Are you asking her or telling her?" Sammy smiled.

"Telling. But I feel bad telling her just like that."

"It's a breakup letter, not a Shakespearian sonnet."

"Right." Joshua exhaled. "Lissa. I'm breaking up with you. I'm in love with someone else. Don't come to Indiana. I won't marry you."

"Ouch. Maybe not *that* much bluntness."

"Do you want to write it for me?"

"Oh, no. This is too much fun." Sammy grinned. "I need some popcorn."

Joshua grunted. "I'm effectively breaking her heart."

"That remains to be seen."

"Let me try again. Hello, Lissa. What I was trying to say in my last letter was that I want to break up. I met someone here in Indiana and I want to pursue a relationship with her. I hope you understand. It isn't anything you did. I just feel like we are not right for each other. Sincerely, Joshua Beachy."

"*Ach*. I guess that'll do."

"What's wrong with it?"

"Nothing. It's perfect. Write it. Send it off. And be

done with the matter."

"Be done with the matter? I feel terrible about it."

"As you should. But the sooner you are done, the sooner she can move on to find happiness."

"Happiness. Okay." He took a calming breath. "This will end in her happiness."

"Eventually." Sammy nodded.

"Eventually."

"Why do you keep repeating what I say?" Sammy chuckled.

"I don't know. I'm nervous, I guess. I just want to do the right thing."

"The right thing."

"Now who's repeating who?"

"I'm teasing you."

Joshua smiled. "I know."

An hour after leaving Sammy's, Joshua slipped his letter to Lissa in the mail. He looked at the time. There were still several hours of daylight left. Maybe today would be the day he'd bump into Susan.

NINETEEN

Joshua had his driver drop him off at the library. He visited there each time he came to town because he was pretty sure Susan would visit the library at least once in a while. Like every other day, he'd searched and came up with nothing.

Last week, he'd gone by the apartments across the street and asked the manager if Susan was renting there. They'd said they couldn't give out any personal information, but he couldn't recall a Susan. Of course, even if there had been a Susan renting, it didn't mean it would be *his* Susan.

He was halfway down the sidewalk from the library when he noticed a woman turn a corner up ahead, heading toward him. As he examined her further, something about her seemed familiar. She was wearing the same outfit as the woman with the cop at the pizza place. What were the odds? He did his best to recall if Susan had any of the mannerisms this woman had.

He was too far away to positively identify her. She was fiddling with something in her hand—a phone, maybe?—so she hadn't looked in his direction yet. Maybe he should step out of sight until she came closer. It would be best if she didn't see him before he tried to speak with her. He had no idea how many Amish men visited the library on a typical day, but he guessed it probably wasn't a common occurrence. He'd stick out like a sore thumb in his Amish clothes and hat and she'd identify him in a second—if it was indeed Susan.

What would he do if he determined it was her? If he called out her name, would she stop and talk with him or run in the opposite direction? *Nee*, he wouldn't do that. He'd step out of sight and follow her at a distance. That way, he could see where she was going. If she went home, he could go knock on the door.

~

Susan had the uncanny feeling she was being followed. Every time she looked behind her, though, no one was there. The feeling was so strong, she'd begun trembling.

She dialed Blaze's number and he answered on the first ring. "What's up, Sue?"

"I hate to bother you, but I think someone might be following me."

"What? Where are you?"

"I'm on my way home from work. I'm near the Tyson Apartments, two blocks from the intersection at the 50."

"Hang on, I'll be right there. Whatever you do, don't go home. Go into the dollar store and wait till I show up. I'm on patrol. I'm going to swing in from behind and trail you to see if I can see anything."

"I'm scared, Blaze."

"Don't be. I'll stay on the phone with you, unless I need to put it down. If I do, you can rest assured your assailant has been apprehended."

"Uh, okay."

"That means I've caught the bad guy." She heard his smile though the phone. "Okay, I see you now. I'm a few blocks down. Don't turn around. Keep walking. Okay, I think I see someone. I'm going to intercept him. I'll stop and talk to him, but you keep walking until you get to the store." Blaze's line went dead.

She heard the slight beep of a siren and turned just in time to see Blaze step out of his patrol car and approach the stalker. Except...instead of stopping to talk to Blaze, the perpetrator ignored him and began jogging toward her.

Oh no!

As soon as she realized it had been an Amish man that Blaze just slammed against the car and handcuffed, Susan began running in his direction.

"Blaze!"

"Stay back," he warned.

"Blaze, no!" She panted. She finally came close enough to realize who it was. "Joshua?"

"You know this man?" Blaze's cautious gaze examined her.

"Susan, I need to talk to you," Joshua pleaded, his glare landing on Blaze.

"Yes, I know him. Please, uncuff him." She touched Blaze's forearm. "It's okay."

Blaze glanced back and forth between her and Joshua. "Is this the *complication* you spoke of?"

She half-smiled. "Yes."

Blaze stared at Joshua, clearly upset. "Why didn't you stop when I ordered you to?"

Joshua's gaze flicked toward her. "I couldn't let Susan disappear."

"Do you realize it's a Class A misdemeanor to evade an officer?"

"*Nee.* I do now." Joshua hung his head.

Blaze sighed and turned the key in the handcuffs. He scrutinized Joshua as he removed them from his wrists. "Are you also aware that stalking is a Level six felony according to Indiana Code 35-45-10-5?"

"Uh, no." Joshua gulped.

Susan realized that Joshua, like she, probably didn't even understand what all that meant, except that it was something bad.

"Since Sue seems to be okay with me uncuffing you, I'm going to let you off with a warning. But know that I will not hesitate to cuff you and throw you in jail if it happens again. Never resist an officer of the law."

Jah, Blaze took his job seriously.

Susan fought a smile.

"I'm sorry, Officer. Our people are usually nonresistant. I just had to talk to Susan."

~

"Well, that was something I never imagined happening." Joshua said wryly as he rubbed his sore wrists, thankful the cop had *finally* left him and Susan alone.

Susan set a mug of steaming coffee in front of him. Although it was warm outside, the temperature inside her tiny studio apartment was cool enough for coffee to be enjoyable.

"In his defense, though, you should have stopped when he told you to. Blaze thought you were a bad guy." She giggled.

He was glad one of them could find humor in this situation. "*Jah*, I've got the bruised ribs to prove it."

"He thought I was in danger." She sat on the edge of the bed, since there was only one chair at the table. "I'm sorry."

"I'm just glad I finally found you. And that I have you all to myself." A heavy breath whooshed from his mouth. "Susan, I want to tell you about Lissa."

"Your *aldi*." She frowned.

"No. I mean yes, but no." He closed his eyes and rubbed his forehead. "Lissa *was* my *aldi*. I left a letter breaking up with her before we moved here."

"You broke up with her in a letter?" She gasped.

"I *would have* told her in person, I wanted to, but she was visiting her *schweschder* in New York. My folks sprung the move on me. She wasn't home when I found out and when we left a week later, she still wasn't home."

"You couldn't have called her?"

"*Nee*. Her folks didn't have a phone number for her." He sipped the hot beverage. "I sent off another letter a couple of weeks ago just in case she didn't get the one I left with her *vatter*."

"Why are you telling me this?"

"Because. Don't you see? My heart was already free when I kissed you. Lissa was part of my past. I always felt that something had been missing between me and Lissa." He stood and walked over to her and reached for her hand. "But that thing that was missing? I found it with you."

"What thing?"

"Love." His eyes beseeched hers.

She pulled her hand away. "I'm not going back home."

"Ever?"

"Not yet. I'm not ready."

"I'm not here to ask you to come home." He sat beside her.

"You're not?" Her eyes searched his.

Ach, he wanted to reach his hand to her brow and erase that worry line. "No. I see that this is something you need right now. I don't know why. And you may not know why. But *Gott* knows why. And I've decided I'm going to trust Him with the 'whys.'"

Her eyes widened. "You are? Really? You're okay with me living *Englisch*?"

"I am. But I want to see you, Susan. Even if you're not ready for a courtship. If you just want to be friends right now, that's okay."

She turned to face him. "What if I don't want to be friends?"

Sorrow gripped his heart, and he hung his head. "You don't want to be friends?" The words emerged as a defeated whisper.

"*Nee.*" Her finger latched under his chin and lifted it, so his eyes connected with hers. A slow smile formed on her lips, and her hand slid up his bicep. "I don't think I can just be friends with you."

He gulped as she inched closer. "You don't?"

"No," she murmured, her lips mere millimeters from his. "I don't."

"Neither do I."

His hoarse words concluded when she leaned forward and closed the gap between them. His hand moved to her head and his fingers seemed to get lost in her unbound hair. Her mouth teased his, until he captured her lips and deepened the kiss. His free hand wrapped around her waist, haphazardly moving her shirt ever so slightly, causing his hand to rest on the warm skin above her jeans. *Ach, Englisch* clothes were dangerous. He'd already noticed the fact that the *Englisch* clothing she wore accentuated the curves that were usually hidden in the confines of an Amish cape dress.

Before he realized it, they had reclined against her

pillows, his lips matching hers kiss for kiss. Susan's love—her passion—equated to pure bliss. Her roaming touch was addicting, like a powerful drug that he craved more and more of. His hands begged to travel, but he forbade them. Not an easy feat.

When he determined they were almost to the point of no return, he forced himself away. "Susan, we can't."

He fought to catch his breath and steady his pulse. It wasn't working. Especially when desire blazed in her eyes. When her hand seared his chest. When her lips found his again.

He groaned. God help him, he didn't want to stop. He couldn't. He never realized how deep his Beachy blood ran, until this moment.

God, if You don't want this to continue, You've got to help me. I'm too weak to resist.

At that moment, a loud knock sounded on the door.

He and Susan both jumped up.

"It's Blaze," she mumbled.

He quickly buttoned up his shirt and raked his fingers through his hair, silently tossing a prayer of thanksgiving heavenward. Susan's cheeks were alive with color and her full lips glistened. *Ach*, she was the most beautiful woman he'd ever seen. Spending his life with her would be a dream come true.

She wrenched open the door.

Except, it wasn't Blaze.

It was Nathaniel.

And her father.

And the district deacon.

Oh, dear. This was not *gut*. Not *gut* at all.

TWENTY

"Susan! What are you doing?" Her father's eyes moved back and forth from her to Joshua. "Joshua Beachy, what is the meaning of this?"

"See, he's known where she's been the whole time. I knew it," Nathaniel said. "That's where he's been scurrying off to every day."

Susan's brow lowered. *Every day?*

"*Nee*, I only found her today," Joshua insisted. His gaze floated to hers, bathing her in a loving caress.

"Right." Nathaniel's word dripped skepticism.

"It's true. This is the first time I've seen Joshua since I've been gone." She hoped it wouldn't be the last. She wanted to capture his hand in hers and pull him close. She wanted to shut the world outside so they could be alone. She wanted more time with this man she'd become wildly crazy about.

"Susan Miller, you must return home," the deacon ordered.

Her eyes flickered toward Joshua, then narrowed on the deacon. "I'm not coming home." She stood her ground with a confidence she didn't fully feel, but Joshua's supporting stance gave her spirit the boost she craved.

"You must come home and repent, or face the *Bann*." The deacon's mien hardened.

"She already said she wasn't coming home," Joshua reiterated. "Do as you must."

"Joshua Beachy, you do not speak for *mei schweschder*." Nathaniel looked like he was having a difficult time keeping his emotions intact. Susan loved her *bruder*, but sometimes, he tended to be a little overzealous toward the Amish ways. He'd likely make a *gut* deacon someday.

"I've already said my piece." Susan nodded, thankful for Joshua's support. "Please leave now."

"We are not leaving," Nathaniel said.

"You will leave, or I will call the police." Susan stared her brother down, but he turned his glare on Joshua. "It's your choice."

"She means it," Joshua said.

"Joshua Beachy." The deacon turned toward him. "If you wish to remain in *gut* standing in the community, you will cut ties with Susan Miller now."

Joshua's mouth fell open and his gaze collided with hers. She was willing to bear the consequences of her actions, but she had no desire to bring her beloved down with her. She shook her head.

"I will risk the *Bann* for Susan," Joshua said.

"Joshua, *nee*. I won't let you," she insisted.

"Fine," the deacon said.

"*Nee*!" Susan cried. She knew being in the *Bann* would prove difficult for her, but living at home in the Amish community would multiply the sorrow a hundredfold. She would not allow Joshua to endure that for her sake. "Wait. I want to speak to Joshua alone."

The deacon eyed her father and Nathaniel and gestured for them to step outside.

Susan closed the door and took Joshua's hands in hers. "I don't want you to be in the *Bann*. You just moved here. You've reunited with your brothers...I don't want you to give all that up. Not for me."

Joshua moved closer and wiped the tears from under her eyes. He brought her near and pressed a kiss to her lips. "I couldn't leave you if I tried."

"Then come stay here with me. It will be too difficult living in the Amish community and being in the *Bann*. At least you'd have me."

"*Ach*, Susan. What will I do here amongst the *Englisch*? I'm a farmer."

She felt for him. No doubt, he couldn't imagine living in her tiny apartment day after day. To her, it was freedom. To him, it would be prison. He'd likely go crazy.

His hand combed through his hair. "Besides, it wouldn't be right, us living here together and not married. We would...do things we shouldn't." He caressed her cheek and a flame flickered in his eye.

He was right about that.

"Then go back. At least, pretend to. Take my number and you can call me. We'll meet in secret if we can manage it." She hurried and scribbled her phone number on a scrap of paper, then thrust it into his hand.

"Like tonight?"

She tugged her lip in between her teeth, thinking of the unrestrained kisses they'd shared before they'd been interrupted. "How did they find out where we were?"

"I have no idea. Nathaniel must've followed me, is all I can guess." He shrugged.

"They'll watch you like a hawk, you know."

"I know. Maybe we can meet at the library occasionally? All I know is that I can't live without you, Susan Miller."

"I feel the same. But you must adhere to their wishes. For now."

An impatient knock sounded on the door.

"*Kumm*. I need one more kiss." He pulled her into his arms and proceeded to bestow the most gentle, yet passionate, kiss she'd ever known.

She'd remember it as long as she lived, along with the forlorn look that flashed across his face before stepping out the door.

Like he was being led to the gallows.

~

"You know, you made a wise decision," the deacon spoke in Pennsylvania Dutch as their driver headed toward home.

Joshua could only grunt. It didn't help that they were in a vehicle that seated five and he was sandwiched between Nathaniel and the back driver's-side door. All he wanted to do was crawl into his bed and forget that the second half of this night ever happened. As for the first half—well, he was sure and certain he'd *never* forget that.

TWENTY-ONE

It had been a week since Joshua had last seen Susan at the motel, but he must've relived their moments together a thousand times. He desired to give her the freedom she sought, but he also worried about her getting too attached to the things of the world. What if she decided she didn't want to come back to their people?

If he were to leave the Amish to join her in the *Englisch* world, he would lose everything. He'd never needed to set aside large amounts of money like his brothers had, because he always knew that as the youngest, he would inherit the farm and be the one to care for his folks as they aged. If he jumped the fence, that responsibility would fall on Justin's shoulders. If he jumped the fence, he would be without cash for a down payment on a home. If he jumped the fence, he'd have to find a way to make a living.

Gott, please let Susan figure things out soon. Until she did, he'd just have to be patient. And content. And patient. *Jah,* not his strong suit.

"Sammy wanted me to invite you to the men's fellowship."

Joshua knew the words, and the invitation, had been difficult for Nathaniel to utter. He didn't like the tension and animosity that pervaded their relationship. How was it that Nathaniel and Jaden got along now? Nathaniel didn't seem to show any hostility to either of his brothers. But him? If he walked into the room, Nathaniel's smile turned upside down.

"Why do you hate me so much?" Joshua challenged him.

Nathaniel's lips twisted. "Hate you? I don't *hate* you."

"Come on. It's obvious to anyone with eyes. I can't even walk into the house without you glaring at me."

"Why do you think? I told you to steer clear of my sister. What did you do? The opposite. Guys like you want one thing. I will not have you bringing shame to my sister and our family. I wish you would just stay away from Susan."

"Why? Don't you want to see her settled down and married?"

"Not to a Beachy."

"So, it's my family you don't like." He stood from the bench and pivoted. "You know, the way I see it is, whether you like it or not, I plan to pursue and hopefully marry your *schweschder*. In the Amish church. That means we will likely be brothers-in-law. You will eventually need to get over yourself and accept me. It is the Amish way.

"I don't know if you read your Bible, but mine speaks of loving not only your neighbor, but your enemy as well. I don't want us to be enemies. If I have done something to offend you, I ask you to forgive me. But know this, whether you choose to or not, I will *not* allow you to make my decisions for me. That is something *Der Herr* has put in my hands. And until He takes that away, I will do what I think is best in my life, according to His will."

Nathaniel swallowed and examined him. "I'm only looking out for Susan."

"*Nee*, I don't think you are. I think you're looking out for your own pride."

"I am not *hochmut*."

"No? You just said in your own words that you didn't want your sister to marry a Beachy," Joshua challenged. "That statement insinuates that you consider yourself better than a Beachy. That is pride. God wants us to esteem others better than ourselves, not the other way around. I have come to you asking for forgiveness, even though I don't think my request is warranted. But just in case I have sinned against you somehow, I have come to you in humility. You could show the same." Joshua took his hat from the rack, and stepped outside, not waiting for Nathaniel to respond. He didn't have all day to try to reason with Susan's *bruder*, and it might be better if he gave him some time and space to think on their conversation. Because while he craved Nathaniel's acceptance, he wouldn't force it out of him.

~

"How did the time with your Amish boyfriend go last week? I never did ask." Blaze cocked a brow as they headed toward his mother's car. Today would be Susan's first day of driving and she could hardly contain her excitement.

She thought on their time in her apartment and couldn't help the slow smile that formed.

"I'll take that as it went well." Blaze chuckled. "Alright, before we start, you need to inspect the vehicle from the outside."

She frowned. "What do you mean?"

"Make sure none of your tires are flat or low. If they are, you need to add air to them."

"That's one thing I never need to worry about with the buggy. We don't use rubber tires in our community."

"Well, you're not in your Amish community now. Okay, if all is well, get in." He handed her the keys.

"You want me to...but I've never..."

"I know. Don't worry, I'm going to guide you every step of the way. Now take a deep breath."

She did as he said.

"You can do this."

"I can do this." She blew out a breath. "But I'm scared."

"I'll tell you what. I'll drive to an empty parking lot and we can practice there. That way, you don't need to worry about running into any cars."

"I think I would like that better." She handed the keys back to him.

"Not so fast. I want you to start the car."

"*Ach*, you're sure?" Her hands shook slightly.

"Okay." He opened the passenger's side and slid into the seat, adjusting it to fit his height. "Go ahead and adjust the seat to where it's comfortable. You'll need to be able to push either of those pedals on the floorboard with your right foot."

"My right foot?"

"Yes. You'll only use your left foot if you're driving

a stick shift. And I don't suspect you'll be driving one of those anytime soon. The adjustments are on the side of the seat."

She moved the seat as he'd instructed. "Now, what?"

"Look at your gearshift and make sure it is next to the P. P is for park."

"It's next to the P."

"Now, put your key into the ignition, turn it away from you just until you hear the engine roar to life, then let it go right away. If you hold it there, you could ruin the starter."

"Ach, I don't want to ruin your mom's car."

He smiled. "You won't if you follow my instructions."

"Okay. Turn, then let go." At his nod, she started the car. "I did it!"

He laughed. "Yeah, you did. You passed the first test. Now, get out and let me drive to the parking lot."

She couldn't hide her smile if she tried. She was actually learning how to drive a car.

As they traveled toward the empty parking lot, she turned toward Blaze. "Will you tell me about your family?"

"What do you want to know?"

"About your wife and child."

174

"Ex-wife."

"What happened?"

He sighed. "You know, I've asked myself the same question many times over." He shrugged. "We were happy at first. But then I was gone a lot because of my job. My job was stressful. When I was home, I just wanted to relax. I didn't want her telling me what I was doing wrong. I didn't have a very good rein on my emotions. I was young and prideful and stupid.

"One day, I came home early and found her with another man." His voice was laced with pain. "It was my best friend. She cheated on me with my best friend. Needless to say, I flew off the handle. Slammed him against the wall. I had to be on leave and almost lost my job because of it."

Sorrow for Blaze gripped her heart. She couldn't imagine his heartbreak. "*Ach*, that's so sad."

"Before the divorce was final, she told me she was expecting my baby. I didn't believe her. I was sure the kid was his. I took a DNA test and it confirmed the truth. All of that was about three years ago. I've only seen my baby a few times. It's so painful seeing my ex-wife, you know? I was in it for the long haul. For forever. I heard she and my friend parted ways last year."

Susan reached her hand to rest on his forearm. "I'm so sorry, Blaze."

175

"Not as sorry as I am." He pulled into the empty parking lot in front of an old, abandoned building.

"Have you thought of trying to mend your relationship? Asking for forgiveness for your part?"

"No. I don't think I can ever trust her again after that."

"But surely the baby needs his father."

"Her. It's a girl." He reached into his pocket and pulled out his wallet. He opened it and showed her a photo. "It's the only picture I have of her. That was a year ago."

"She's precious. You don't want to try to work things out? For her sake?"

He worked his jaw. "I don't know. In a way, I do. In another way, I'm worried it will just add more turmoil to her life."

"*Jah*, but you said you were young and hot-headed. Have you not changed since then?"

"I'd like to think I have." He tapped the dash. "Okay, enough about me. It's time for you to drive."

She hesitated, not ready for the conversation to be over. "Blaze, will you consider my words?"

"I'll consider your words, Susan." He'd been calling her that since he'd heard her real name from Joshua's lips. He said he preferred it. She didn't mind either way.

She opened the car door and moved to the driver's seat. "Let's do this."

TWENTY-TWO

Sunday meeting had been a difficult one for Susan's family and Joshua. Just hearing the decree about Susan's excommunication sent a shiver up his spine. While he generally loved the ways of his people, this was one thing he did not.

He'd refrained from making contact with Susan because he knew his actions were being observed. Hopefully, Susan understood his lack of communication. He'd already decided that he wouldn't make a phone call to her unless he was visiting one of his brothers in their community. Calling her from the Millers' phone shanty presented too much risk.

If the warning from the leaders hadn't been enough, his father had cautioned him to abstain from a courtship with Susan. But in his mind, it was too late. He knew in his heart she was the one *Der Herr* had chosen as his life mate. He'd just have to wait for His perfect timing to bring them together.

~

Susan removed her apron and joined Blaze at one of the small tables in the café. She enjoyed her *Englisch* life, truly, but she missed Joshua more than she cared to admit. If Blaze and his folks hadn't been present in her life, she'd be crazy with loneliness.

Blaze tapped on the table. "You've got fifteen minutes for your break?"

"*Jah.*"

"Good. I have news to share with you."

She smiled. She liked when Blaze had good news. If he ever had bad news, he never shared it with her. And for that she was grateful. "What is it?"

He sucked in a breath. "Well." He blew it out. "I took your advice. I contacted Renee. We're meeting at the park today and she's bringing Adelaide with her."

"*Ach*, Blaze. That's wonderful!" She took a sip of her sweet tea.

"It's just a baby step. But...I mean, I'm not a praying man. But would *you* mind saying a prayer for me? That the Man Upstairs lets it go well?"

Tears pricked her eyes. "Of course. Yes, I will. But you can pray too."

"I might try that." He reached for her hand. "Thank you. I have a good feeling about this. For the first time in a long time, I have hope."

"Blaze." Susan smoothed away a tear. "I'm so happy for you." She wouldn't tell him, but she would be praying for more than just the reconciliation of his family. She'd pray that he'd also be reconciled to *Der Herr*.

"So, what's going on with you? Heard from your boyfriend lately?"

She shook her head.

"Are you worried? It's been, what? Over a week, right?"

"Almost two. I'm sure they've already placed the *Bann* on me, which means he's forbidden to continue a relationship with me."

"I think I might be worried." He sipped his frappé.

"I'm sure he is just being careful. He said he would contact me when he could. Right now, I'll just have to trust him."

"So, what do you plan to do?"

"What do you mean?"

"Well, if he's there and you're here, and your relationship is forbidden..." He shrugged. "I mean, you can't expect the guy to wait for you forever, right?"

"Right. I don't know. I haven't figured it out yet."

"Did you decide what you want to do about your driving permit? Have you thought more on getting a Social Security card? We've been doing all this driving. If you had already applied for a permit, we could be logging your hours in."

"*Jah*, I know." She sighed. "I'm just not comfortable with the government knowing everything about me. And I would have to go to my folks and get my birth certificate." She shook her head. "It just sounds like a big headache."

"I kind of understand, but what we've been doing is against the law. Not really a smart move for a cop. You know what I mean?"

"You want to stop giving me driving lessons, then?"

"If it's not leading to anything, what's the point?"

Susan sighed. Blaze was right. What was the point if she wasn't going to get her license? She'd thought that was what she wanted, but now? She just wasn't sure anymore.

If Blaze did reconcile with his *fraa*, which she hoped he would, their days of hanging out together were numbered. The thought saddened her heart.

"Well." Blaze looked at his watch and stood from the table. "I'd better let you get back to work." He pointed to her before opening the door to leave. "I'm counting on your prayer."

She nodded and waved as he shimmied out the door.

Gott, *please work in Blaze's heart. Please help him not only today, but in the days and weeks and months ahead. Draw him to You and help him to find the joy he needs in his life and heart. Amen.*

TWENTY-THREE

Joshua was out in the garden harvesting tomatoes when he heard his father call his name. He set his bushel aside to see what the urgency was all about. *Daed* looked like he was heading back from the phone shanty. Had something happened? Had they finally found a place of their own to buy? *Ach*, Joshua prayed it would be so.

But as *Daed* neared, it wasn't excitement Joshua recognized in his mien. It was devastation.

"What is it, *Daed*? What's wrong?" Alarm jolted through his body.

"It's your *aldi*."

"Susan?" His heart pounded so loudly he could barely hear his own word.

"*Nee*. The one in Pennsylvania. Lissa Lambright."

He frowned. "What about her?"

"You might want to sit down."

"Just tell me, *Daed*."

"She is in the hospital. They don't know if she's going to make it." *Daed* stared at him, his gaze communicating sympathy. "She tried to take her own life, *sohn*. They found an empty bottle of pills on her bed. Along with the letter you'd sent."

"*What*? She..." Emotion filled him as the truth of what *Daed* had just told him began to register. "*Nee!*"

He had known that Lissa was the emotional type. But never in a million years would he have thought she'd react to their breakup this way. "That's terrible." His hand splayed over his face, and he couldn't stop tears from forming.

Daed pulled him in for an embrace.

"What should I do, *Daed*?" He cried on his father's shoulder. "Should I go visit her?"

Daed moved back and shook his head. "I'm not sure the family would want you there."

"I feel awful, *Daed*. Like I should do something."

"You can pray for her."

He shook his head. "This is all my fault. If I would have just gone over there and talked to her in person..."

"You cannot blame yourself for telling her about your true feelings toward her. You had no way of knowing she would react this way. You are *not* responsible for her actions, no matter what may have provoked them. *She* chose that path. You did not."

"But she could die." Once again, he broke down. The weight of the matter settled heavy on his heart. He had no idea how to make this right.

~

At the knock on the door, Susan checked the peephole. Blaze was still working, so she didn't expect him to be visiting at this hour.

Nathaniel?

She pulled the door open.

"Susan, you need to come home. Now."

TWENTY-FOUR

The only person Joshua could think of to talk to was Sammy. He had so many questions that needed answers. Mainly, why?

Sammy ushered him inside the house and provided him with a glass of lemonade.

"I believe that everything *Der Herr* does, everything He allows, will ultimately bring Him glory. His Word says that His ways are perfect." He squeezed Joshua's shoulder. "We may not understand it all, but we can trust that *Gott* does."

"I don't know why she would do something like this. And over me? I'm just baffled by the entire ordeal. I feel so bad. What if she dies? I don't know if I'll ever be able to forgive myself."

"You cannot place that blame upon your shoulders."

"My *Daed* said as much. But I can't help but feel like I'm to blame."

"Do you know if your former *aldi* ever trusted Christ as her Saviour?"

He shook his head. "I don't know. What would it even matter? I mean, if she were to die by suicide..." he shrugged. The hopelessness of it all was downright disheartening, depressing.

"It matters a great deal. It's a matter of Heaven and Hell."

"But I thought...if she were to commit suicide, to murder herself basically, how could she repent of that? Doesn't the Bible say that murderers will not enter the kingdom of God? That they will go to hell?"

"Tell me something, Joshua. Do you think Moses is in Heaven?"

"I would think so."

"You know that he was a murderer, right?"

"*Ach*, I hadn't thought of that."

"What about King David? Or the Apostle Paul, who wrote most of the New Testament? Do you think they're in Heaven?"

"Yes."

"Murderers. Both of them."

Joshua scratched his head. "Yes, but they probably repented before they died."

"So, is that the prerequisite for Heaven? To repent before you die?" Sammy's eyebrow arched.

"Well, kind of. We have to place our faith in Jesus."

"That's right."

"And what happens when we do that?"

"He saves us?"

"For how long?"

"Well, the Bible says that when we believe in Jesus, He gives us everlasting life."

"How long does everlasting last? When does it end?"

Joshua frowned. "It doesn't. It's forever."

"Right. So, if your former *aldi* had accepted Christ, and she had killed herself, everlasting life wouldn't apply to her? So, you're saying we are only saved until we sin again?"

"I don't know."

"Well, if that were the case, *Der Herr* would only be saving us temporarily. It would be called temporary life, not everlasting." Sammy reached for his Bible. "I want to show you something."

"Okay."

"Read this verse." Sammy pointed to 1 John 3:9.

"*Whosoever is born of God doth not commit sin; for his seed remaineth in him: and he cannot sin, because he is born of God.*" Joshua looked up at Sammy, his mouth hanging open. "Wait. What?" He read the verse again. This time, quietly.

"That is right."

"But I have been born again, and I still sin."

"Yes. It also says in the same book that if we say that we have not sinned, then we are liars. As long as you are living and breathing on this earth, your flesh will sin. But here is the key: it is your spirit that is saved and sealed until the day of Christ Jesus. Your spirit cannot sin because Christ dwells inside of you."

He reached for the Bible. "Let me read a couple verses to you. The first one is in chapter ten of the book of John. It is Jesus speaking. *And I give unto them eternal life; and they shall never perish, neither shall any man pluck them out of my hand. My Father, which gave them me, is greater than all; and no man is able to pluck them out of my Father's hand.*" Sammy looked up at Joshua. "Did you get that? Nobody can take you out of His hand, if you belong to him. He keeps you safe."

"I see."

"Paul said, *I know whom I have believed, and am persuaded that he is able to keep that which I've committed unto him against that day.*"

"So, God is our Keeper."

"That is exactly right. He keeps His children safe in His hand until He brings them home."

"But what about our sins?"

"They are covered by the blood that Christ shed on Calvary. That is what grace is all about. It is something we can never earn, so God gives it freely."

"But if we know that our sins are already paid for, doesn't that give us a license to sin?"

"God forbid, is what Paul says. Sin is bondage. Why would you go back into bondage once you've been set free? I want to live a *gut* life for *Der Herr* because I am grateful for what He has done for me. Jesus said, *if ye love me, keep my commandments*."

"So, in a sense, we are to be keepers too."

"You can put it that way." Sammy stared at Joshua. "I guess the question now is, do you know if your former *aldi* is saved? And if she isn't, what are you going to do about it?"

"I have to tell her, Sammy. She needs to know about Someone worth living for. I need to go to Pennsylvania."

TWENTY-FIVE

The week in Pennsylvania had zapped all of Joshua's energy and all he could dream about was coming back to Indiana, finding Susan, and holding her in his arms. *Bann* or no, he needed her in his life. At this point, he was ready to give up his standing in the Amish church to be with her.

After being with Lissa, he realized how fragile life was. He didn't want to do life without Susan. Precious moments were being wasted, all because he was forbidden to see her. No more. He'd had enough.

Instead of dropping him off at home, he instructed his driver to head into Versailles. He hadn't called, so she would be surprised to see him, for sure.

He stood outside her door, poised to knock, when a male voice called from behind him.

"May I help you, sir?"

He turned, eyeing a man who appeared to be a

janitor, he guessed. "I don't think so. I just came to see my girlfriend."

"Susan Miller?"

Maybe the man was the motel manager? "That's right."

"She doesn't live here anymore. Moved out a few days ago."

"What? Where did she go?"

"I couldn't say." He shrugged. "Maybe she couldn't afford the rent and went to live with her cop friend?"

Her cop friend. Right. *Ach*, he'd had a bad feeling about him from the first—and only—time they'd met. Of course, that might have had more to do with his ribs cracking against his patrol car.

"Okay, thank you." Well, that was a dead end. Too bad he hadn't brought her phone number with him. He'd been in such a hurry to leave for Pennsylvania that he hadn't thought things through. And he wouldn't dare call the shanty and ask someone at home to locate it for him. Since she was in the *Bann*, they'd likely confiscate it to never see the light of day again.

It's a *gut* thing he'd asked his driver to wait.

His hope deflated, he opened the car door. "Could you just take me home, please?"

~

Susan's heart flip-flopped the moment she heard the vehicle heading down the driveway. Although she ached to run and throw herself into Joshua's arms, she refrained. Instead, she adjusted Nathaniel's straw hat on her head and continued to attach wet laundry to the line. Joshua would find his way to her soon enough.

Not ten minutes later, his tall frame sauntered toward her.

"If I'm not mistaken, that looks like Susan Miller, doing women's work." His teasing tone tugged a smile from her lips.

She foisted a hand on her hip. "Women's work, huh?"

He snatched a pair of pants from the basket and fastened them to the line. "I've missed you. What are you doing here?"

"Last time I checked, I lived here." Her grin widened. "I moved back home."

"For *gut*?"

She shrugged. "For now." She enjoyed teasing him too much.

"What do you...?" His worried brow melted her heart, and she ached to kiss his anxiousness away.

"Well, I don't plan to live with my folks forever, you know." She pulled her bottom lip between her teeth and caught his inquisitive gaze.

He reached for her hand and drew her behind one of the sheets she'd hung from the line. He brought her close and stared down into her eyes. "*Nee.* I wouldn't want you to live with your folks forever." His hand brushed a stray hair from her face. "How would you feel about moving out this fall?" he murmured.

"This fall?" Her eyes widened. "I don't know." She tapped his lips with her finger. "I suppose a woman could be persuaded. How about winter? That'll give us more time to prepare."

"Winter?" he muttered. "I suppose I can wait that long if I *have* to."

A loud throat clearing caused him to release her from his embrace.

"Nathaniel? Do you need something?" Susan narrowed her eyes at her *bruder*.

"I'm just making sure this Beachy is behaving himself," Nathaniel's gaze moved back and forth between them.

Joshua grunted.

"He just got home. Give us some privacy, please." Susan pointed at Nathaniel. "And stop being a busybody."

Nathaniel waved a hand, turned around and headed the other way.

"I swear, he hates me," Joshua mumbled as Nathaniel walked off.

"He doesn't hate you. The day you left for Pennsylvania, Nathaniel showed up on my doorstep in town. He told me what had happened with Lissa and said you really needed me."

Joshua's eyes flew wide and he gestured in the direction her brother had disappeared to. "He— Nathaniel—did?"

Susan smiled at the surprise in his tone. "I think he might be warming up to you, *ain't not*?"

"I can't believe it." He shook his head. "Is *that* why you're here?"

"Partly. It was time to come home, I realized. I went and talked to Bishop Bontrager and told him I planned to stay in the community. He talked to the leaders and they lifted the Bann."

"*Ach*, that's *wunderbaar*."

"I pretty much had everything I'd wanted in the *Englisch* world. I was living on my own. I had a job. I learned how to drive a car."

"You did?"

"*Jah*, Blaze taught me."

"*Ach*, Blaze. The police officer." Distaste saturated his words.

"He's a *gut* guy. Really sweet. The best kind of friend."

Joshua's lips pressed together. "I don't know how I feel about that."

"Blaze has a family, Joshua. A *fraa* and a *boppli*."

"What? He does?"

"*Jah*. They are divorced." She frowned at the sad word that represented a broken home and broken dreams. But *Der Herr* was the mender of broken homes and broken dreams.

"I see."

"*Nee*. I don't think you do."

"What do you mean?"

"Well, I encouraged Blaze to try to make amends with his family and to forgive his *fraa* for leaving him. I'd been praying for him, for *Gott* to heal their relationship. Anyhow..." She had to fan her eyes so emotion wouldn't seep between her lashes.

"What?"

"He met with her. She said that she'd started going to church and she found Jesus. *Gott* changed her heart. She had been praying for *Der Herr* to right the wrongs she'd done in her life." She reached for Joshua's hand and blinked back her tears. "Blaze said he was going to church with her this Sunday. Isn't that *wunderbaar*?"

"*Jah*, that is *gut*. Maybe *Der Herr* will work a miracle for them."

"I'm praying for it." She nodded. "Joshua, I feel like that might have been my whole reason for leaving our people and going to the *Englisch*. I think *Der Herr* arranged it that I would meet Blaze and that we would help each other find *Gott's* will for our lives."

"Wow, that's...incredible." His thumb roamed over her hand. "I need to tell you about Lissa."

"I heard." Susan frowned. "Is she okay?"

"She is now. They are going to try to help her. The doctors think she may have a hormone imbalance that makes her extra sensitive. But the best part in all of it is I got to talk to her about *Gott*."

"What do you mean?"

"I asked her if she knew for sure that she would have gone to Heaven if she had died. She said no. I was able to tell her about *Gott's* love and His *wunderbaar* grace, and that He wanted to live inside her and fill the empty space in her heart. She'd thought that I had been the missing piece in her life, but the real missing piece was Jesus. Now, she is whole."

"I think we have both seen a miracle."

"There's more than two. I got a miracle too." He pulled her into his arms, leaned down and sweetly kissed her lips. "I found the love of my life."

EPILOGUE

Susan's vision moved from table to table as happiness filled her heart. Her entire family was present at her and Joshua's wedding and laughter floated through the air as her older *brieder*, Silas and Paul taunted each other. Her *schweschder* Emily rocked a brand new *boppli* in her arms while her husband Titus encouraged their other *kinner* to eat. Next to them sat their niece Bailey, expecting her and Timothy's second child. Her face glowed just as much as Susan's, she suspected. Joshua's *brieder* Josiah and his family; and Jaden, Martha and the twins; along with Justin, who'd recently arrived in their community all shared a table. Justin had been one of Joshua's side sitters, along with Nathaniel—the two most eligible bachelors in the community now.

Susan and Joshua learned that Nathaniel's change of heart had a lot to do with their wise elderly friend,

Sammy. He had reminded Nathaniel of the passage in
1 John 4 that says, *If a man say, I love God, and hateth
his brother, he is a liar: for he that loveth not his
brother whom he hath seen, how can he love God
whom he hath not seen? And this commandment have
we from him, That he who loveth God love his brother
also.* Nathaniel had approached both Joshua and
Susan with a repentant heart, and they happily
granted him forgiveness and asked him to be an
honored participant in their wedding day. Susan had
a feeling her brother and her new husband would
become *gut* friends.

Joshua reached for her hand under their corner
table, the *Eck*, and squeezed gently. Would anyone say
anything if they sneaked a kiss behind the beautiful
wedding cake her sister-in-law Jenny had made them?

Her smile widened even further as some of their
Englisch guests made their way toward their table.
Blaze, hand-in-hand with his *fraa* and their *dochder*,
approached, offering their congratulations. His face
glowed as he informed them another *boppli* was on the
way. Susan breathed a quite prayer to *Gott* for His
gifts of second chances. The verse about *Gott* healing
broken hearts and binding wounds came to mind.

Behind Blaze's family stood a line of well-wishers,
including Sammy Eicher, his *gross sohn* Michael and

fraa Miriam, along with their clan. Susan could hardly believe how much everyone had grown over the years and she suspected their *kinner* would be beginning families of their own soon.

She also wondered if some of the older folks present might soon be retiring to their eternal rewards in Heaven, a bittersweet thought, indeed.

One thing she knew was that she had complete confidence in *Der Herr* and trusted Him to guide all their lives as He saw fit. His ways were perfect. She and Joshua had agreed as one to place their hopes and dreams for the future in the hands of *The Keeper* of their souls.

THE END

Preorder the next book in the series NOW!

The Pretender (Amish Country Brides)

It was only supposed to be a pretend courtship. That was the deal. It hadn't included a kiss.

Amy Troyer was shocked when her fiancé supposedly left her for the *Englisch* world two years ago. But now he's back, and rumor has it he's engaged to a woman from another Amish district. With her sister's upcoming wedding and holiday festivities being planned, the last thing Amy wants is to show up dateless. So, she hatches a plan to not only make her ex jealous, but to silence the pitiful stares from family and friends.

At first, Nathaniel Miller balks at the idea of pretending to be Amy Troyer's significant other, but he admits he'd like to axe his brothers' teasing. As the two of them get acquainted and spend more time together, though, he finds himself falling for his *schweschder's* best friend.

Could it possibly be *Der Herr*—instead of Amy— orchestrating their fake courtship?

Releasing **November 9, 2021**, Lord willing!

Dear Reader,

I hope Joshua and Susan's story brought a few smiles to your face. I loved writing about Joshua's meetings with Sammy. Because Sammy is diligent in his study of the Word, he is able to help others in their struggles. I encourage you to study God's Word too so it will be a lamp unto your feet and a light unto your path, and so you can find answers to anything life throws your way.

Blaze was a bit of surprise character in this book, but I'm glad he shared his story with us. No matter where you are in your life, whether on a mountain or in a valley, you can know that God is ready and waiting to help you. All you need to do is reach out to Him; as we read in the book of James, *draw nigh to God, and he will draw nigh to you.* He loves you and wants to help!

Blessings in Christ,
Jennifer Spredemann

Thanks for reading!
Word of mouth is one of the best forms of
advertisement and a HUGE blessing to the
author. If you enjoyed this book, **please** consider
leaving a review, sharing on social media, and
telling your reading friends.

THANK YOU!

DISCUSSION QUESTIONS

1. Joshua is upset because, even though he isn't as invested in the relationship as Lissa is, he knows breaking up will hurt her. Have you ever refrained from doing something because you thought it would be painful for someone else?

2. Joshua and his family moved to a new state. Have you ever relocated with your family to another state or country? How did you feel about it?

3. Susan hadn't expected the Beachy family would be living in her home. Have you had another (unrelated) family move into your home before?

4. Susan is annoyed with Joshua at first, but as she gets to know him, she discovers they have an easy friendship. Have you ever misjudged someone who later became a friend?

5. Do you think Nathaniel's cautiousness is warranted? Why or why not?

6. Susan is determined to leave her community because she feels she is missing out on something. Have you ever felt that way?

7. When Susan enters the *Englisch* world, she quickly discovers she's inadequately prepared for her new life. Have you experienced anything similar?

8. When Susan first encounters Blaze, she is nervous. Do you feel nervous around officers of the law?

9. Although Blaze is hurting inside, he still reaches out to others with kindness. Are you able to see past your hurts to help others?

10. When Joshua is in the throes of temptation, he mentally pleads for God's help, which he receives immediately. Have you ever called out to God and found help in your time of need?

11. Have you ever known anyone like Lissa?

12. In the story, God brings forgiveness, hope, and healing to several characters. How has God helped you?

A SPECIAL THANK YOU

I would like to express a *special* thank you to all my readers, who helped with the names in this book. To reader **Nancy Winn**, thank you for suggesting "Nancy" for one of the twins. And thanks to **Dawn Creal, Barbara Beechy, Carol Welch,** and **Linda Herold** for giving the book its name *The Keeper*.

I'd like to take this time to thank everyone that had any involvement in this book and its production, including my Mom and Dad, who have always been supportive of my writing, my longsuffering Family—especially my handsome, encouraging Hubby, my Amish and former-Amish friends who have helped immensely in my understanding of the Amish ways, my supportive Pastor and Church family, my Proofreaders, my Editor, my CIA Facebook author friends who have been a tremendous help, my wonderful Readers who buy, read, offer great input, and leave encouraging reviews and emails, my awesome Launch Team who, I'm confident, will 'Sprede the Word' about *The Keeper*! And last, but certainly not least, I'd like to thank my *Precious LORD and SAVIOUR JESUS CHRIST,* for without Him, none of this would have been possible!

If you haven't joined my Facebook reader group, you may do so here:
https://www.facebook.com/groups/379193966104149/

Made in United States
Troutdale, OR
09/28/2024

23190393R00137